OUT OF STEP

JANE CORBETT

Beggar Books

First published in 1986 by William Collins Sons & Co. Ltd
Second edition published in 2022 by Beggar Books

A CIP catalogue record for this book is available from the British Library

ISBN: 978-1-910852-81-1
eISBN: 978-1-910852-80-4

Cover image and design by Jamie Keenan
Typeset by yenooi.com

1998

1

END OF TERM

"Oh, before you go, Fleur, Mrs Miller wants to see you in her office after school today," Miss Winthrop said brightly, refusing to catch Fleur's eye. Miss Winthrop never liked to get involved with anything she suspected had to do with unpleasantness. If someone behaved rudely she simply ignored it, hoping, no doubt, to make them feel ashamed. Since this never worked, her classes frequently descended into a sort of free for all, with everyone shouting at once and no one listening. Sometimes Fleur felt sorry for her, but on that day the smug way in which she delivered her message put any such consideration out of her mind. Miss Winthrop gathered her books together.

"That'll do for now, everybody. Go and get changed. *Quietly* now!"

Her voice was drowned by chairs scraping and desks banging as the class began to shove its way out of the room.

"Who's Mrs Miller's pet Flow-er, then?"

Jim Forbes leaned forward and stage-whispered into her ear, with a hopeless attempt at a Welsh accent. He sat at the desk behind Fleur's and the mention of her name always aroused some sort of comment from him, like pressing the bell for Pavlov's dog. Jim Forbes had recently put on a sudden spurt of growth which, together with the appearance of a faint, whiskery down on his chin, made him think himself a force to be reckoned with by the female sex. He stretched one leg forward so that he could run the toe of his trackshoe up and down the back of Fleur's calf. She turned round on him in fury. He was wobbling his head on his skinny neck and leering at her, with a look that she presumed he took to be sexy. It actually made him look like one of those silly nodding dogs some people keep in the back windows of their cars.

"Just shut up, Big Mouth," she hissed.

He leaned back in his chair and said in the authoritative tones of the Headmaster, "I'm afraid you're just going to have to shape up or ship out, Materson, my girl."

Betty, who was sitting next to Fleur, giggled. Jim grinned at her and, gathering his books up under his arm, swaggered out of the classroom.

"God, I can't stand that posturing creep!" Fleur said furiously. "He'll probably make Head Boy in a couple of years. Just the type!"

"He could do worse. So could the school!" Betty said frostily and walked off towards the door.

She's *touchy!* Fleur thought to herself, hoping that it wasn't because Betty was falling for the Forbes charm. She couldn't seem to find the right tone with anyone these days. *This whole term seems to have been one aggravation after another,* she thought, *and to cap it all I've got to see Mrs Miller at 4 o'clock. Thank God it's nearly the summer holidays. In a week we'll be in Corsica.* It was to be her first trip abroad, and the prospect of it shone like a beacon on the horizon of her otherwise messy and dreary life.

AT FIVE PAST four she was standing outside the door of Mrs Miller's office. On the surface Mrs Miller was all sweetness and feminine charm. But underneath Fleur knew her to be pure flint. She took a deep breath, arranged her face into a blank expression, and knocked at the door.

"Come in," called a soft, reasonable voice.

She went in.

"Ah, Fleur, take a seat. I shan't keep you a moment."

Fleur looked round for the chair which was furthest from the desk and sat down. Mrs Miller was going through a pile of reports and signing them. Every now and then she sighed and shook her head in patient resignation, before adding her signature with a flourish. She was a mistress of the theatrical gesture. Fleur glanced round the room while she waited. Its impersonal, institutional look had been transformed by Mrs Miller's little touches of domesticity. There were carefully tended pot plants on the desk and window sill, a tray with real china cups and teapot, a reproduction of one of Degas's dancers on the wall, and Mrs Miller's pink coat hanging neatly on a hanger behind the door. A sweetish, talcum-powdery smell hung in the air.

I wonder what Mr Miller's like. A humble little man, tidied away into his armchair in front of the TV, rarely allowed to move in case he makes a mess. He probably even has his meals there; TV dinners served up still in their foil containers, that don't require the fuss of cooking or washing up, and can be fitted into one of those special trays in beige plastic that attach to the arm of your chair. Poor bloke! A fellow prisoner, only his is a life sentence.

Mrs Miller replaced the cap on her fountain pen, folded her hands on the desk in front of her, and fixed her attention on Fleur. "Now, Fleur, why don't you pull your chair a little closer? It's rather difficult having a conversation with someone who's so far away, you know."

Fleur shifted her chair an inch closer. Mrs Miller sighed and pulled a report out of the pile. She glanced through it then looked up again.

"I have here your end of term report, and I felt that in all fairness I should have a little talk with you before sending it to your mother." She paused to see the effect of her words. There being no response from Fleur, she continued with a resigned air. "Next term you enter the Fifth Year and have your O levels exams and C.S.E.s in front of you. One or two of your teachers say that you are not without ability, but what about this: Maths, 'Inattentive in class'; Social Studies, 'Could do much better... Spends too much time daydreaming out of the window'; German, 'Less attention on the boy behind, and more on her work, might have made this term less of a waste of time.' I'm afraid that unless there is a radical change in your attitude, you're not going to have much success in the future. You see, I am the one who has to decide which set to place you in for next term."

Fleur kept her face in a fixed expression but there was a rising feeling of nausea in her stomach.

"I didn't get on very well with my German teacher. It was mainly a misunderstanding…" she mumbled.

Mrs Miller cut her off. "It's not a question of who in your opinion you do or do not get on with, Fleur. It's a question of buckling down to some serious work and showing yourself to be altogether more mature and cooperative. I've been keeping a close eye on you over the last couple of years, and I'm bound to say that what I've seen doesn't inspire me with much confidence. Even your insistence that you wanted to play the saxophone didn't come to anything. You've got to learn to stick at things."

"I *did* stick at the saxophone. It wasn't my fault I had to give it up. I didn't have anywhere to practise, and then Mr Fish had to stop coming because of the cuts…"

"Ah, yes, the cuts! Anything can be blamed on them, can't it? But if you'd been *really* determined, ways would have been found."

"That's not what I was told."

Fleur felt close to tears but she wasn't going to let Mrs Miller see that she'd got to her. It had been like this between them ever since Fleur had come to the school, a year later than everyone else. The reason for that was that after her parents had split up when she was five years old, her mother had taken her to live on a communal farm in Wales. They had not returned to London until Fleur was almost thirteen. She'd hated London after the rambling farm and the wild, beautiful hills of Wales. She hated its greyness and the dinginess of their cramped flat. But worst of all was school. In Wales she had attended the village school. It was a small, friendly place run by two elderly sisters, and all the children were taught together in one big classroom. The elder sister taught the older children and the younger taught the little ones. Sometimes Fleur and one or two of the older children helped with the little ones, which she always enjoyed (the other children at the farm were all younger than her), and there was always lots of singing, hymns and old Welsh songs, accompanied by one of the sisters on the harmonium.

Then suddenly Fleur had found herself in a school of twelve hundred pupils, doing subjects she'd never heard of, like Information Technology and European Studies. She stuck out like a sore thumb from the other kids, who laughed at her scruffy clothes and Welsh accent, and called her mother "Hippy". One day one of the school football stars broke his leg on the pitch and had to go to the hospital. The girls in Fleur's class decided to send him a huge Get Well card, and each of them had to write a message in it. When it came to Fleur's turn, she had no idea what to put.

"Do I have to? I don't even know him," she pleaded. But they insisted.

"Just say, 'Hello Gorgeous, from an Unknown Admirer!'" giggled one girl.

"No, I'll tell you what to write," said Fat Margot, and proceeded to recite a very rude limerick which caused them all to fall about in fits of laughter. Margot's Dad ran a pub and she was always full of hilarious jokes and stories.

Everyone agreed that this was just the thing for Fleur to send and stood around watching and giggling as she wrote it down. With every word she wrote, she felt worse, but their acceptance of her was still too shaky for her to dare to refuse. Finally the thing was sent off but never reached the boy it was intended for because it was intercepted by Mrs Miller. Mrs Miller, shocked by the obscenity it contained, took it straight to the Headmaster, and Fleur, together with her mother, were summoned to an interview. The Headmaster asked Fleur if she had anything to say to explain her disgraceful conduct. But what could she say? That she's been made to do it by the other girls? That wasn't even strictly true. So she said nothing, and Mrs Miller had taken that as further sign of the general hardness of her character. Later she'd tried to explain to her mother, who thought that the best thing was probably to say no more about it and let the incident blow over. The trouble was that for Mrs Miller it never had blown over.

"So, after considerable thought," Mrs Miller said, "I've decided to move you down a set for next year, at least to start with. Your progress will be carefully monitored and if you do well you will be moved up again. I hope you will look on this as a challenge. Have you anything you wish to say?"

Fleur had plenty to say, like whether Mrs Miller thought that picking on her all the time and branding her as a failure was really likely to encourage her to do better? But she didn't trust herself to speak without giving away her feelings. She looked down and said in a surly tone, "What do my other teachers say?"

"They've been consulted of course. I have to admit that, well, not all of them thought it was the best course. But on balance there was agreement, and in any case the final decision always has to be mine. Adolescence is a difficult time and you have a number of crucial decisions in front of you. It is my job to try and ensure that you make the right ones. I assure you I am only thinking of your welfare, Fleur."

Like hell you are! You think I'm the bad apple that'll rot the whole barrel if you're not careful, Fleur thought, but she said nothing.

At least some of her teachers had stuck up for her, and she knew who they would be. Mr Parker, the English teacher, and Miss Macnamee who taught Arts and Crafts and never had any trouble in her classes because everyone enjoyed them and wanted to work.

Mrs Miller stood up from her chair, fixing Fleur with her concerned, serious look.

"I hope you'll think over what I've said to you during the holidays, and come back next term with a thoroughly positive attitude. That'll be all for now, Fleur. Close the door behind you, would you please."

Fleur stood up and, with a mumbled "Thank you," shuffled out of the office. As she pulled the door to, she heard a ruffling sound behind it and thought with satisfaction that it must be Mrs Miller's pink coat falling off its hanger.

She walked fast down the corridor, taking deep breaths to get rid of the acute feelings of anger and frustration that an interview with Mrs Miller always produced in her. She was certainly not going to spend her summer holiday thinking about Mrs Miller's criticisms or trying to develop a "positive attitude". She was going to wipe school from her mind, do nothing but sit on a hot beach in Corsica, drinking in the sun and enjoying the pleasures of life. The thought of Corsica reminded her suddenly of Jan, who would have been waiting for her at the school gates for the last half hour. She broke into a run, dived into the cloakroom for her jacket and school-bag, and dashed out of the building.

Jan was Fleur's closest friend and, like her, something of a social oddball in their school. Her father was an MP and her elder brother was about to go up to Cambridge. The family, however, believed in state education and all three children had been sent to local schools. Jan herself wasn't particularly clever or in the least stuck up and, in addition to her having a pleasant, easy-going personality, she was slow to take offence so had been quickly accepted by the other kids. Fleur liked her because she had a good sense of humour and spoke her mind. She also enjoyed going to Jan's house. It was big and roomy, always full of people who dropped in for a drink and a chat at any time of the day or night. They sat around, talking and drinking wine with Jan's Mum, in a kitchen that resembled something out of a glossy magazine only more lived in, and smelled of garlic and wine stews; very French. The Taylors were keen on France and often took a house in the Dordogne for the summer. But this year they had decided to do something different.

"We're going to Corsica and we'd love for you to come along too," Mrs Taylor had said. "Johnny's off to Crete with his pals, and Tony's not much company for Jan, being only thirteen. Besides, they bicker all the time when they're left on their own. You'd be doing us a real favour if you came along, and it might even improve your and Jan's French before the O levels!"

Fleur had jumped at the idea. With the amount she could save from her Saturday job and what her mother could give her, she could just about afford it. The Taylors, with characteristic generosity, had at first expected nothing but the fare from her. But Fleur's mother had insisted on making a proper contribution to her upkeep so in the end they'd given way. Fleur had spent six weeks drawing up lists of what she needed to take with her, and trying to imagine what the little town where they were staying would look like and whether she would be able to see the sea from her bedroom window.

"Its going to be fantastic!" she said to Jan.

"Let's hope there's some entertaining local talent," Jan said. "It's a good time I'm going for. Stuff the O level French!"

JAN WAS PACING up and down outside the school gates.

"What the hell've you been doing in there?" she exclaimed as Fleur panted up to her.

"Honestly, I'm sorry you had to wait so long. I was having the thumbscrews turned by Mrs Miller," Fleur said.

"Oh God, what did the old harridan want this time?" asked Jan, forgetting her annoyance.

"She's putting me down a set next term, for my moral improvement."

"Still trying to turn you into a normal, decent person, is she? Well, she'll never get away with it. Once you're in the Fifth Year you'll be out of her clutches. You'll see, there'll be plenty of other teachers who'll stick up for you."

"I hope so."

"'Course there will. Horrible old cow! Anyway, forget her. This year's almost over. Come on, I'm starving. Let's go and get some chips."

She linked her arm in Fleur's and they set off down the road. Fleur was already feeling more cheerful as she always did in Jan's company. She began to describe the interview in more detail, including her vision of Mr Miller in his telly chair and the fall of the pink coat. Jan laughed, delighted, and by the time they reached the chip shop, Fleur had got rid of her anger and was able to look at the whole incident more philosophically.

"I just wish I could think of the perfect cool reply that would shut her up for all time."

"No one ever manages that. Except perhaps for Oscar Wilde, and it didn't do him much good."

"Didn't it? He must have got some satisfaction out of it."

Jan laughed.

"Perhaps. He was another misfit, like you."

They bought their chips and wandered into the newsagent's next door to browse amongst the magazines. The shopkeeper eyed them with distaste and in a few moments told them rudely to get out if they weren't going to buy anything, and take their filthy, greasy chips with them. Out on the pavement once more, Fleur remembered that she'd promised to do some shopping for her mother and that it was nearly closing time.

"I've got to dash. See you tomorrow," she said.

"OK. And take it easy!" Jan called after her retreating back, as she dashed off in the direction of the bus stop.

FLEUR'S MOTHER was already home when she got there. She was in the sitting room on her hands and knees, surrounded by a sea of cloth, cutting something out. She looked up and smiled.

"Oh, hallo, love. I'm just cutting out a dress for your holiday." Fleur's heart sank. She peered at the colourful material more closely, trying to prevent the alarm from showing in her face. When she was little she had loved the dungarees and pinafores, embroidered with brightly coloured animals or fruit, that her mother had made her. But now that she was older she scarcely had the heart to tell her mother that she'd much rather go to the shops for her clothes, like everybody else her age. Her mother was one for making everything, a true child of the sixties. Partly she did it because they never had any money to spare but also she enjoyed it, and Fleur had to admit that in many ways she was very talented. She even made some of their furniture, though that too had its drawbacks and embarrassments, like chairs that collapsed beneath people and neighbours pretending not to recognise their abandoned cast offs, which her mother had found in the street and brought home to renovate.

"Oh, great," she said, more enthusiastically than she felt. "Is there a picture of it anywhere?"

Her mother tossed her up the pattern. It wasn't as bad as she feared. Just a simple sundress, and no doubt the material wouldn't look so bright under the Corsican sun.

"I thought, you've got nothing to wear when it's hot, and then I saw this lovely material in the market. It seemed just the thing with your colouring. What d'you think?"

"Yes, it's fine," Fleur said. Then, feeling suddenly ungrateful, she leaned down and kissed the top of her mother's bent head. Her mother had beautiful hair, dark chestnut that curled naturally into silky waves and tendrils. Her own hair was more of a carroty colour and never seemed to lie down properly.

Her mother looked up happily. "I'm so glad you like it. Fancy a cup of tea?"

"Yes, I'll go and make it," Fleur said, picking up the shopping and carrying it into the kitchen.

Her mother had been busy in there too. Beside the pile of still unwashed breakfast dishes, were small bowls of chopped fish and vegetables marinading in peculiar smelling sauces. Her mother had recently gone in for Chinese cooking and the elaborate preparations suggested that Frank was expected for supper. Frank was her mother's boyfriend and as far as Fleur was concerned, a thorough pain. He was from California and though he was younger than her mother, he behaved to Fleur like some old hippy uncle, telling her all about how great various antiquated rock groups were and the reasons why the student revolution of '68 had been doomed to failure. She wasn't the least interested in either of these topics, nor in his passion for someone called Buckminster Fuller and his geodesic dome, all of which he lectured about as a visiting teacher in the Art School where her mother taught print making. Her mother said that what she found so refreshing about Frank was his enthusiasm, but it was obvious that she found him sexy and had simply fallen for his prehistoric hip style. Fleur just wished that she'd admit it and stop going on about what a worthwhile person he was if only Fleur would give him a chance.

She washed up the dishes while the kettle boiled, then made the tea and carried it into the sitting room. She handed one mug to her mother and said airily, "By the way, don't bother to cook for me tonight. I had something on my way home."

"Oh, but I'm making something special, and Frank's coming round."

"I'm not hungry. Besides, I've got things to do."

"But won't you just have a bite with us? Frank and I are probably going to the movies later, so you'll have plenty of peace and quiet then." The tone of her voice betrayed her hurt but that only irritated Fleur further.

"Leave it out, Mum. I've told you, I don't want anything." She picked up her schoolbag and made for the door. In the doorway she turned back and said, "Have fun at the movies. They say you're only young once!"

Inside her room with the door closed, she immediately regretted being so bitchy. She didn't really begrudge her mother her new found happiness. It was just that she wished she wouldn't try to include her in it, make them into some happy little threesome. All she wanted was to be left alone.

She went over to the chest of drawers and stared into

the mirror that hung on the wall above it. The face that stared back was scowling and sullen, framed in a shock of woolly red hair. Who could possibly care for such a disagreeable creature? She turned away miserably and lay down on the bed. She had to do something about herself, take herself in hand, stop getting involved in useless battles at school, stop taking out her frustrations on her Mum. Perhaps after Corsica it would all be different. She would come home a changed person, ready and determined to make a success of her life. She stared up at the picture of Ben Webster on the wall opposite her bed, this month's portrait in the jazz calendar her mother had given her for Christmas. He was old and frail by the time the picture was taken but from the rapt expression on his face, with its wrinkled brow and distended cheeks, and the delicate placing of his old man's hands on the gleaming brass stem of his tenor sax, she knew that he had lost none of his mastery.

If she closed her eyes, she could hear the sound he made, like on the record she had, a sound that stirred her in the pit of her stomach and made her get goose flesh on the backs of her arms. He was dead now, but his music lived on just the same. One day she'd take up the sax again and learn to play it properly. She'd never be able to play like Ben but that didn't really matter. She'd play well enough to give herself, and maybe even a few other people, some pleasure.

2

ON THE TOWN

On Saturday morning Fleur woke with a familiar start of panic. She was late as usual, must throw on her clothes, clean her teeth, and run like the clappers if she was to avoid another detention. She was half way out of bed when she remembered that there was no more school. She sank back into the warmth and comfort and closed her eyes. But her inner clock was too geared to the 8 a.m. scramble to get back to sleep, and after half an hour of tossing and turning, she decided to get up. She might as well make a cup of tea, rather than lie there getting more and more restless.

The flat was silent as the grave. She remembered that her mother had got a weekend conference at her college, and must already have left. It still made her feel peculiar to find herself alone in an empty flat. Time seemed to stand still in the ringing silence, as if she was the last person left on earth. In the kitchen beside the pile of last night's supper dishes, there was a note under the honey jar. It was sticky and when Fleur opened it, something fell out. She read, "Had to dash. Here's a couple of quid to buy yourself something nice for lunch. See you tonight. Love, Mum. X."

She made tea, left the washing up, and wandered into the sitting room. She cleared a corner of the sofa to make room amongst the sewing and the newspapers, and sat down. She sipped the hot tea and tried to think about what on earth she was going to do today. The wonderful sense of release she ought to have, at that moment felt more like a vacuum. What was she going to do to fill in the time before going to Corsica? She'd made her lists of what to take weeks ago. All that remained in way of preparation was the last minute washing and ironing. Outside the summer sky was grey, a slightly paler version of the peeling houses in the terrace opposite. There wasn't a patch of green in sight — except the dusty, greenfly-ridden petunias that her mother tried to coax to life in the windowbox. She hated London, especially in summer. In Wales the green hills would be full of harebells and plump cushions of flowering moss. And the changing sky was always on the move, ribbed mackerel clouds meaning a change in the weather, or thick cumulus riding high over the hill tops, piling up into fantastic towers until suddenly a gleaming shaft of light broke through like the finger of God. There would be mountains in Corsica too, she supposed, but not green ones. The colours there would be brown, red and yellow, earth colours, and there wouldn't be any clouds. She hunched over the tea, mug between her cupped hands, trying to picture it all.

When she had drunk her tea, she went back into the

bedroom and turned on the radio. But after ten minutes of nothing but the disc jockey's cheery morning chat interspersed with inane phone calls from listeners, she switched it off. She sat down in front of the mirror. Her face looked what her mother would call "peaky", surrounded by its wild mop of hair. She picked up her brush and attacked her hair vigorously in an effort to render it smooth and silky. Piling it up on top of her head, she turned her face from left to right, studying the effect. Then she let it go and turned from the mirror in disgust. If only she was naturally beautiful — the sort of girl she'd seen in a movie thriller about foreign correspondents, camera and travelling bag slung over one shoulder, casually elegant, as she strode across the runway to the waiting plane that was to take her to an assignment in Managua or Jakarta. That was the sort of life she dreamed of. She rummaged in a drawer for a clean teeshirt, dragged on her jeans and slopped into the kitchen to tackle the washing up.

She was just putting the last of the plates away, when the phone rang.

"Hi, sluggabed!" Jan's voice said. "Watcha doing?"

There were voices and laughter in the background. Jan must be phoning from her kitchen.

"Sluggabed? I'll have you know I've been up for hours slaving away at the pigsty in our flat. Mum's out. How about you?"

"Well, if you're hoping to get the Victoria Cross for domestic drudgery, that's not what I called about, I'm afraid. What I want to know is what you're going to do when you've finished?"

"I haven't gotten round to thinking about that. Why, have you any suggestions?"

"Certainly have. How about this? Some people are going to the Rock Palace tonight, and I thought we might go along too. There's the Mean Machine playing and it's a terrific place."

"Sounds great. The only thing is, how much does it cost to get in?"

"A couple of quid, not much. I'll sub you if you're skint."

"No, that should be OK. Mum left me a couple of quid for lunch."

"Well, I'll stand you a drink when we get there. Great. See you at the tube station at 7.30, then. And don't be late. I hate hanging around there on my own."

"No, I won't. Promise. See you later."

"See you. Bye."

Fleur hung up. Already the day looked altogether brighter.

In the late afternoon Fleur decided to have a leisurely bath and wash her hair in preparation for the evening. She was still lying in the steaming water, reading a magazine, when she heard the front door open and close. After a few moments her mother put her head round the bathroom door.

"Oh, there you are love. Had a good day?"

Her mother looked tired, as if her day hadn't been particularly rewarding.

"Yes, fine. How about you?"

"Oh, so, so. I need a cup of tea. D'you want one?"

"Thanks. I'll be out of here in a minute. I've got to meet Jan."

"Oh, you're going out? That's nice."

"Yes, we're going to a club up town with some friends."

"Well, don't be back too late. And make sure you come back with Jan. I don't want you coming home late on your own."

"It's OK, Mum. Don't worry, I won't."

Fleur had already returned to her magazine. Her mother's warnings were a familiar recital. Anyone would think she was about twelve years old and didn't know a thing.

Her mother left and she went on reading, feeling very relaxed in the hot steamy bath. She must have dozed off for a moment because she came to with a start to find her magazine soaked, swollen and unreadable, except for a couple of lines at the bottom of each page. She threw it onto the floor where it landed with a wet slap, and got out of the bath.

In her bedroom she dried herself and rifled through the drawers in search of something to wear. There was another clean teeshirt, a blouse she'd bought at a jumble sale and never worn, a couple of sweatshirts, one of which she'd grown out of, and a spangly chainmail vest. She picked out the vest to go with the new skirt, very short and tight, that she'd just bought with her Saturday pay, and her favourite red shoes. She dressed, put a little makeup carefully round her eyes, brushed out her hair, and went into her mother's room to study the effect in her long mirror. There stood a tall, rather tarty-looking girl, small prominent breasts clearly visible through the chain-mail, hips tightly hugged by the short red skirt, and long exposed legs. She rushed back into her room and tore everything off again. Half an hour later she was still sitting on her bed surrounded by every garment she possessed, having decided that she'd better phone Jan and tell her that she wouldn't be able to make it after all, when her mother came in to the room with a cup of tea and a sandwich.

"I thought you'd better have this since you'll miss supper," her mother said, her eyes alighting on the sea of clothing. "Good heavens, it looks as though a bomb's dropped! Have you been trying on your whole wardrobe?"

"Only because I've got nothing to wear," Fleur snapped.

"What about that silvery vest and your white jeans?"

"Oh, Mum, nobody wears jeans to discos any more!" Fleur felt close to tears. "And anyway you can see my tits through that vest."

"D'you want to borrow my body stocking? It's in the drawer, clean."

"That's no good," Fleur wailed, close to despair.

"Please yourself. But at least eat the sandwich," Fleur's mother said and left the room.

Fleur ate the sandwich, though she didn't feel hungry, and drank the tea. Then she fetched the body stocking, put on the vest, white jeans and red shoes, grabbed her jacket and purse, and dashed out of the flat, calling goodbye to her mother. She was late as usual, and Jan would be furious.

· · ·

THE DISCO WAS ALREADY CROWDED when Fleur and Jan got there. It was a converted cinema, with the seats taken out but all the thirties style decorations left and repainted in sophisticated colours, like crushed raspberry and pistachio green. Beneath the stage there was a dancing area. Above it, to one side, the disc jockey was suspended in a gilded cage. In between records he rapped out a stream of smart talk, directed largely at the group of girls who clustered round him, hanging onto the bars of his cage. A few people were dancing but most were standing about in groups. Conversation was almost impossible above the pounding music. Jan and Fleur made their way to the bar, which was situated at the back of what used to be the stalls. It was a bit quieter there and there were some tables and chairs. They bought a couple of shandies and sat down.

"Well, we're part of the 'in-crowd' here, all right," Jan said.

"I'll say."

They peered into the gloom, fitfully punctuated by gyrating shafts of coloured light. The clientele were certainly exotic, dressed in everything from army fatigues to dinner jackets, thirties style, and net tutus. There were heads of glossy, slicked back hair, and others brilliantly coloured like parakeets and decorated with spiky stars or stiff coxcombs.

"At least it's better than the old Roxy, don't you reckon?" Jan said. "My God, I've never seen so many trendies gathered together in one place!"

"This must be, as the Standard says, 'what living in London is all about!'" Fleur said.

She was enjoying herself and rather wished they weren't due to meet a whole crowd of Jan's friends. She only knew a couple of them and didn't feel particularly at ease in their company. They seemed so much older and more sophisticated, and yet in other ways more childish too. Very soon, however, they began to arrive and because the music made talking quite difficult, Fleur didn't feel as awkward with them as usual and was even glad that together they made up something of a group. It gave her confidence in the face of so many extraordinary beings.

When the band came on, she forgot everything else in her excitement. The Mean Machine was one of the best hard rock bands around and at once everyone was up and dancing. Fleur loved to dance and when she was moving, caught up by the rhythm, all senses drowned in the pulsating sound, alone, yet linked to all the other mobile bodies on the floor, she felt entirely happy. From time to time she glanced at Jan or another of their group gyrating next to her, and grinned happily. When the set was over, she returned to their table near the bar, hot and exhilarated. Seated at their table, she noticed a good-looking boy of about nineteen who hadn't been there before. When she went up to the bar for a couple more shandies, she found him standing next to her. He leaned on the bar on one elbow, waiting for her to be served first. He was well dressed without being showy, and altogether striking. When she glanced at him, he caught her eye and gave her an amused grin.

"Let me get those," he said, pointing to the glasses she offered to be refilled.

Fleur blushed and said, "Thank you," hoping that since

her face was already flushed from dancing, he wouldn't notice the blush.

"Do you always move around in convoy?" the boy asked.

"Not really. It's the first time I've been here," she said, not quite understanding what he meant and feeling that he might be making fun of her.

"Never mind," he said. He paid the barman and picked up the drinks.

"Let's sit down where it's a bit quieter and you can hear yourself speak."

He led the way towards an empty table near Jan's, handed Jan her drink and sat down next to Fleur.

"My name's Hugh. And yours?"

"Fleur."

"Your mother obviously has a literary bent."

She only just caught what he said, but this time she understood it.

"Er, yes. After the heroine of *The Forsyte Saga*. It was serialised on TV about the time I was born."

Hugh laughed in a friendly way. "I wonder if you'll live up to her?" he said above the hubbub.

"Don't know much about her. Was she nice?"

"Oh, yes. She enjoyed herself." He smiled again. He had a lovely smile, Fleur thought, only she wasn't sure what he was thinking. She rather liked that. At least he wasn't totally predictable like Jim Forbes.

"Great, isn't it?" Fleur said, indicating the assembled company. "Have you been here before?"

"Several times. I prefer Quigs though. Smaller, and the people there don't have to try so hard."

"Are they trying hard here?"

She wondered if he meant just their appearance or their effort to enjoy themselves.

"Never seen so many posers in my life. Have you?" Hugh said.

"I suppose not." *He certainly knew his way around,* she thought. "What sort of music do you like?" she asked.

"Jazz and blues mainly. I play sax."

"Do you? I've always wanted to do that. I did learn for a bit but then the teacher left. It wasn't easy to practise in our flat either."

Hugh smiled sympathetically. "It's a pretty fulsome instrument, the sax. What d'you play now?"

"The record player."

They both laughed.

"I expect you're very good," she said.

"The band I play with have got a gig on Friday night at Frolics. You should come along."

"Thanks. Perhaps I will."

This was the sort of thing she dreamt about. She'd heard of Frolics but even Jan hadn't been there as far as she knew. Perhaps they could go together. She could hardly wait to tell her about it. She'd known from the first that there was something special about Hugh.

The band came back on stage for the second set.

"D'you want to dance?" he asked.

"OK."

She got up. On their way to the dance floor, she saw Jan notice them with a look of surprised interest. She felt very proud that for once she wasn't a wallflower but had been singled out by one of the most striking boys in the place.

Hugh could dance as well as she had somehow expected he would. His movements had a natural grace and fluidity. Fleur gave herself up to the rhythm, moving in concert, close but never quite touching him. She was on top of the world. A few moments later she felt a tap on her shoulder and Jan's voice bellowed in her ear, "You're doing all right for yourself, I see!"

Fleur grinned at her and went on dancing.

For the next couple of hours she and Hugh danced and chatted together during the breaks for refreshment. He told her about the gigs he'd played in Holland and France, and how they'd been chased out of one town after they'd plunged the hall they'd been performing in, plus fifty of the neighbouring houses, into total darkness by over-loading the circuit. They'd ended up having to sleep in the van, and when they woke up in the morning, had found themselves marooned in a smoking wasteland with even the tyres of the van beginning to smoulder because they'd accidentally parked in the town dump.

"But in the next place, we were looked after like super-stars, the real V.I.P. treatment. That's life on the road for you. Always unexpected, whatever else," Hugh said. She could hardly believe that she was sitting there chatting away with someone who was virtually a rock star and who seemed to be enjoying her company almost as much as she did his. When eventually she happened to glance up at the clock above the bar, she saw to her dismay that it was after eleven. She and Jan would have to go soon if they were to catch the tube. She looked round to see if Jan was at the neighbouring table but there was no sign of her. Eventually she spotted her on the dance floor, gyrating wildly with a tall black boy who was a very good dancer. She turned back to Hugh.

"I've got to go soon," she said.

"Have you?"

He sounded surprised rather than sorry. She wondered if he was going to say anything about their meeting again or remind her about Frolics on Friday night. She waited, hoping that he would do so. After a pause, he said, "It's stuffy in here. Shall we go out for a breath of air?"

"If you like. But I mustn't be long," she said, pleased that he wanted a few minutes alone with her before she had to leave.

He led the way through the crowd, leading her by the hand. Passing the dance floor, she paused to yell to Jan to meet her outside in ten minutes. Then she and Hugh were out in the street.

It had been raining and the streets were wet and shiny. The smell of petrol fumes hung in the air but the city felt very alive. They turned right past a parade of shops, walking hand in hand. A bit further on, between the closed shops, there was an amusement arcade still open, with a cluster of tired, sleazy-looking people and a few kids, punching away at the machines as spaceships exploded silently in mid air and bullets whined from behind cactus plants. Above the entrance the illuminated words, LO 'S OF FUN glowed mournfully in the orange light. At the end of the shops a dark alley ran off to the right. Hugh turned down it. After a few yards the street lamps petered out but Fleur could see enough to make out that the houses were mostly derelict. A piece of newspaper, weighed down with the grease of chips, wrapped itself round her ankle then flapped away. It wasn't a very romantic spot.

A large house formed the blind end of the alley. It had once been grand and traces of its former elegance remained in the elaborate stucco work that decorated its crumbling porch and window frames. Hugh led her up the steps and leaned her back against the sagging front door. The sound of the traffic was faint now and in the dripping stillness, she heard his breathing quicken. Then suddenly he was pressing his full weight hard against her, trying to wrench open her lips and teeth with his tongue. His hands ran roughly over her body, shoving their way into her clothing. She heard the chainmail rip and felt him tugging in frustration at her body stocking. He was panting hard now and cursed in exasperation at the unexpected resistance of her underclothing. For a moment Fleur was paralysed. Behind his bullet head, she read the words, SPURS RULE OK scrawled in paint on the wall opposite. Then she snapped into life. She wrestled and fought against his mouth and hands. Outrage more than fear drove her, that he should dare to take her down this sordid alley and set about her like this. What the hell did he take her for? Surely this wasn't all their evening together had been leading up to? She'd thought him something special and he'd seemed to really like her. Now he was behaving as if all that had never happened, as if he didn't know who she was and didn't care, like some sort of sex maniac. She pushed at him with all her might, twisting her face away and kicking out wildly in the hope of getting his shins. In the end she must have succeeded because he suddenly let go of her and stood back, grimacing in pain. His face was red and puffy and there was a long scratch down his left cheek.

"You vicious little bitch," he said thickly. She pushed him aside and starting to move cautiously round him and backwards up the alley.

"I'm going now, and don't try to stop me." She hoped her voice didn't betray the fear she felt.

"Go on then. D'you think I care? You're nothing but a stupid child," he said, rubbing his shin.

She turned away and began to walk more quickly, pulling her clothes to rights and buttoning up her jacket as she went. Her legs felt like jelly and her cheeks burned with anger and humiliation. At any moment she expected him to grab her from behind, but he didn't. As she reached the open end of the alley, she heard him shout after her, "You're just a bloody little tease, that's what you are!"

She rounded the corner without looking back. Let him shout what insults he liked, she was safe now. But she felt terrible. It was all so sordid and depressing. For such a good evening to end like this! She was a complete fool! How could she have so misjudged things? Ahead, in the distance, she could see Jan pacing up and down outside the entrance to the club. She ran to meet her.

"For goodness' sake, what have you been doing all this time?" Jan said, as she caught sight of her. "We're going to miss the blessed tube if we don't get our skates on."

She grabbed Fleur by the arm and propelled her in the direction of the tube station.

The gates were just closing as they shot through and

ran down the escalator. The train was already standing at the platform and they scrambled in and collapsed onto the seats of an almost empty carriage.

"Phew! That was lucky! We just made it," Jan said. Then, taking in Fleur's dishevelled appearance for the first time, she added, "My God, what's happened to you? You look as if you've been dragged through a hedge backwards!"

The expression of shocked amazement on Jan's face was so funny that in spite of her shakiness, Fleur collapsed in laughter. In a moment they were both helpless with giggles, to the mild curiosity of the elderly couple at the other end of the carriage. When at last the fit began to die down, Fleur said, gasping, "I don't know why I'm laughing. I almost got raped back there."

"You're not serious? You mean that good-looking bloke you were dancing with all night?"

"That's the one. I thought he was a friend of yours?"

"Never seen him before. But what happened?"

"He took me down an alley and virtually assaulted me."

"No! What did you do? How did you get away?"

"I fought him off, kicked him in the shins. I don't think he'd have had the guts to actually *do* anything."

"Well, thank God for that! But what a swine! He was so good-looking too. Honestly, you can't trust anyone these days."

"He seemed so nice. I mean, we spent the whole evening together, talking and everything. You don't expect people to suddenly behave like that."

"I'm not so sure. There's something a bit odd about 20 year old blokes picking up 15 year old girls."

"Even so, that doesn't mean they're all rapists."

"Well, what else do they want young girls for? Their scintillating conversations?"

"I don't see why not."

"Come off it! Anyway, you know what I mean."

"I suppose so. But it wasn't even his grabbing me like that I objected to most, as the place. It was all so sordid."

"Well, it's over now, thank God, and no harm done. Chalk it up to experience." Jan pressed her arm comfortingly.

Fleur nodded, then added mournfully, "He played the saxophone too."

Jan laughed.

"Honestly, Fleur, you're totally naive! Don't you know, musicians are the worst!"

Fleur decided that she wouldn't tell Jan about Frolics. Not that she had the slightest intention of going there now.

By the time Fleur reached home it was after midnight. There was a light on in the hall but the flat was silent. Her mother had gone to bed. She crept along the landing, past her mother's slightly open bedroom door.

"Is that you, Fleur?" her mother's voice called out softly.

Fleur stopped and put her head round the door. "Yes, Mum. Sorry I'm late."

"I'm glad you're back. I was beginning to worry. Did you have a good time?"

"Yes. Well, so, so."

"Oh. Anyway, better get some sleep now. Goodnight, love."

As Fleur's eyes grew accustomed to the darkness, she made out the collapsed uppers of Frank's boots beside the bed. Then she noticed the tousled form of his head on the pillow, snuggled against her mother's shoulder. She muttered a frosty 'Goodnight' and pulled the door to.

In her own room she undressed by the light from the streetlamp, not wanting to catch sight of herself in the mirror or look at her spoiled clothes. She left them in a heap beside her bed with all the other strewn garments. She pulled the bedclothes up to her chin and lay staring out into the semi-darkness.

Was the problem just that she was naive, like Jan said? It was true that she had never had a proper boyfriend. In Wales she'd hardly seen any boys of her own age, and since she'd come to London the only boys she'd been at all interested in were fifth or sixth formers, who never even looked at her. The boys in her class either behaved in a stupid, childish way most of the time, or were posturing creeps who thoroughly fancied themselves like Jim Forbes. So where was she to get that experience from? Her mother and Frank? Perhaps she would meet someone in Corsica. She dreamed of someone darkly romantic, witty, daring and a bit dangerous, like Lord Byron. There was a picture of him, dressed in Albanian costume, in the front of a book of his poems her mother had. She'd always liked the look of him. The Corsican men might be a bit like that. But whatever they were like, at least they would be different.

3

ABROAD

They were bouncing along the straight road from the airport in a rickety light blue bus. Inside the bus there were a few tourists like themselves, none of them English, and some local women, laden with bundles, including a live chicken tied up by the ankles which squawked and flapped across the aisle with every lurch. Outside, the blinding sunlight seemed to bleach the colour out of the brown hills and green patches of trees and vines, even out of the sea which glinted and sparkled in the distance under a white sky. It was midday and the bus was filled with the stifling smell of animals and sweat.

In another half hour they had reached the coast, and began the steep descent into a small town. The bus ground into a low gear and screeched and roared its way round precipitous corners, scattering children and laden donkeys, until it came to rest in a dusty square.

"Phew! Thank God!" Jan said. "Any more jolting around in that stench and I'd have thrown up."

They stood about in the square whilst the driver climbed onto the roof of the bus and deftly threw down the luggage to waiting boys, who distributed it to its owners for a small tip. Fleur's throat was dry from excitement as well as dust. She could hardly believe that they had arrived at last, and blinked round at the blinding light in an effort to take in her surroundings.

The houses that bordered the square were tall and close together, built in a brownish stone, the colour of the hills. There were narrow gullies dividing them and sometimes a flight of steps. Above their tiled roofs, the long, flat bulk of a church loomed.

Jan's father tipped a boy for the last of their bags.

"Right, now. Has everyone got their personal effects? Good. Then let's go and find this flat."

"I've got a map of the town here, Gerry," Jan's mother said. "It looks as if from the square we take the first left leading away from the church. Soon after the Post Office there's another little church and our house is just beyond that. Look, there's even a public washing fountain!" She pointed to the tourist map. "I wonder if it's still used?"

"Well, that's one job you can strike me off the rota for. It's only the women who go to the washing fountains," said Tony, Jan's younger brother.

"Oh, I see. You think you've just arrived in male chauvinist's paradise, do you?" Jan said, sarcastically.

"Well, when in Rome… you know." He sniggered.

"God, I can see *he*'s going to be insufferable," grumbled Jan. Her mother laughed and put her arm through hers.

"Come on, don't start. We've only just got here."

Jan sniffed dismissively. They all picked up their bags

and set off across the square and into the sudden cool of a narrow street.

"Case not too heavy for you?" Jan's father asked Fleur.

"It's fine, thanks, Mr Taylor."

"*Gerry*, please, Fleur. You can't go on calling us Mr and Mrs Taylor for the next two weeks."

"Gerry," Fleur muttered, a blush reddening her already hot face. She didn't know why she found it so terribly embarrassing to call the Taylors by their Christian names.

They arrived at the house exactly according to Mrs Taylor's instructions. It was a four storey building like all the others in the street, with a tiled roof and shuttered windows. A heavy outside door led into a cool courtyard which was entirely filled by an enormous fig tree. From there a peeling staircase led up to their flat on the top floor. Inside the flat there were four large rooms, a bathroom and a kitchen big enough to eat in. From the kitchen window, Fleur could see over the rooftops to the glittering sea. The floors of the rooms were tiled and they were rather bare, giving an impression of space and coolness. What furniture there was, was old-fashioned and heavy, and there were some antique flower prints on the wall and a couple of pictures of saints in the hall, with pale faces and eyeballs lolling heavenwards as if they were in some sort of trance or agony. Above each bed a dried palm frond had been stuck behind a wooden crucifix. The bathroom looked like something out of a museum. The bath was short and deep with huge brass taps and a shelf inside for sitting on because you couldn't fit lengthways. It stood on a sort of dais on lion's feet, and the lavatory too was on a platform with a wide mahogany seat like a throne. Fleur loved the flat though it wasn't exactly the English idea of comfortable. She loved its smell which reminded her of the inside of her grandmother's huge wardrobe; a mixture of lavender bags, clean, ironed clothes, and the slightly fusty, spicy smell of old wood.

They quickly settled into a routine. In the morning Jan's parents got up early and had breakfast, then went off by themselves for a couple of hours. Usually Tony went with them. When Jan and Fleur got up the flat was pleasantly empty and silent. They breakfasted on the coffee that had been left on the stove for them, and dark local bread and butter and delicious apricot jam. In Fleur's experience coffee had always been a rather bitter, tan coloured liquid, drunk on special occasions. This coffee was rich and dark and they drank it several times a day out of small, thick china cups with plenty of sugar that came in big white blocks in a blue box. After breakfast they walked round the town, sometimes stopping off at a café, or strolled to the beach. Lunch was back at the flat at two, omelettes or a big salad with plenty of garlic and some local salami. In the afternoon they went to the beach, and after supper the whole family took a stroll either to a café in the main square or out beyond the town past the Legionnaires' camp. Fleur had always had very romantic ideas about the Foreign Legion, but there was little that was romantic about gloomy barracks, surrounded by a high wall topped with barbed wire and guarded by savage dogs. It looked more like a prison than a fort. On the whole Fleur preferred the route that took them down past the harbour with all its wonderful fishy smells, and the scent of sardines grilled over charcoal that came from the restaurants. These hot, foreign smells, like the scent of dark tobacco and aniseed in the cafés, thrilled her and made her more aware than anything else that she was was in a strange, exotic place.

She loved the market too, and had never seen such an array of fish and vegetables or so many kinds of sausage and cheese. She liked shopping with Jan's mother, who spoke to the stall holders in French which the Corsicans spoke with a heavy accent and rolled Italian 'r's. They were often given free samples of things to taste, thin slices of ham or cheese, an apricot or an olive.

At the flat everyone took a share in the household chores, though Fleur and Tony, being less skilled at cooking than the others, were largely confined in the kitchen to chopping onions and washing lettuce. Mealtimes in the Taylor household were taken with an almost religious seriousness, and much as she loved all the good food and cooking, Fleur did find it at times rather irritating. If her mother had been there, they wouldn't have been able to keep a straight face at such solemnity on the subject of lettuce and olive oil.

The Taylors were very much a family and that too was something Fleur wasn't used to. They did a great deal together and what they did separately, they came home and described to one another shortly afterwards. And they really liked each other, even Jan and Tony, despite their squabbling. There was a pleasant, secure atmosphere in their household, though Fleur did sometimes find it a little stifling, such as when Jan's mother came into their room every night to kiss them both goodnight. In the company of her parents, Jan was still very much their little girl, and Fleur sometimes found herself most in sympathy with Tony, who was more often in the doghouse for some piece of rudeness or uncooperative behaviour. He was an interesting boy, she thought, and unusually easy to talk to for someone of his age.

On their fourth evening Jan brought up the question of the town disco, and they decided to pay it a visit after supper. The disco was a local café that had been converted for the tourists. A wooden platform had been erected at one side of the café, covered by a cane roof. Strings of coloured lights were hung in the roof and in the trees that bordered it, and tables and chairs had been placed on the beaten earth around the platform.

"I think it's got rather a rustic charm despite it's primitiveness," Jan said loftily as they entered.

"Well, it's certainly packed," Tony said, and rushed to grab one of the remaining tables. He sat down and they all followed suit.

Beyond the circle of lights, the soft southern sky was peppered with stars. Inside it, a babble of voices and loud music declared that everyone was having a good time. The customers were all foreign tourists except for a handful of local boys who hung around on the far side of the dance floor, instantly recognisable by their reserved manner and style of dress. A disc jockey, in tight satin trousers and shirt open to the waist, entertained the people between records with a stream of light-hearted chitchat delivered in French and German. As usual, they appeared to be the only English in the place. That was one of the advantages of this part of Corsica, Jan's mother said.

"Let's enjoy the place before the chip-eating hordes

arrive." It was the sort of remark that made Fleur feel rather uncomfortable.

Mr Taylor ordered a bottle of wine and Fleur turned her attention to their neighbours at the next table. They were a large group of fat, jolly Germans, who continually roared with noisy laughter and kept up a boisterous interchange of jokes with the disc jockey that clearly made them the life and soul of the party. This was not, however, to the approval of their neighbours on the other side, who also appeared to be German but of a wholly different sort. They were slim, elegant and restrained both in appearance and behaviour. They made a pointed effort to ignore their noisy compatriots, which Fleur and Tony found quite amusing. They were just observing them, when one of the local boys broke away from his group and approached the sophisticated Germans' table. He stopped in front of their very pretty daughter and muttered something which Fleur didn't hear but which was obviously an invitation to dance. The girl replied with cold embarrassment, not smiling or meeting his eyes, whilst her parents turned away, talking to one another as if the Corsican boy wasn't there. The boy flushed and turned on his heel swiftly, walking back in the direction he had come, a stiff, proud expression on his face.

"Did you see that?" Fleur said to Tony.

"Yes. How can they stand being here if they get treated like that?" he said.

"Presumably they aren't always."

"Once'd be enough for me," Tony said.

Back now with his group, Fleur saw the Corsican whisper something and cast a mocking glance at the

Germans. His friends laughed but their expressions were not very mirthful.

"I think it's disgusting. After all, this is their country," Fleur said.

"They probably don't have much respect for us either, what with all the make-up our girls wear and the smooching with boys in public and all that."

"Yes, you hardly even *see* their girls, except occasionally out shopping with their mothers. What a life!"

"Wouldn't suit me, I can tell you."

"It wouldn't be so bad for *you.* You're a male."

"You don't have to tell me," Tony said, putting on a deep voice and beating his chest. They both giggled.

Fleur was distracted by a nudge from her other side.

"Don't look now, but see that boy standing over there by the record player? Dishy, eh?" Jan said.

"You mean him?" Fleur said, pointing in his direction.

"Keep your voice down and stop pointing," Jan hissed, grabbing her arm.

"Sorry. Yes, I see who you mean."

"I really fancy him. He's German. I heard him talking to someone, but speaks English. I wonder if I could get him to dance with me?"

Her eyes were shining and her white dress showed off her tanned skin and sleek dark hair. She looked lovely, pretty enough to get anyone she wanted, Fleur thought.

"I'm sure you can. Just give a few encouraging smiles in his direction."

She did and in about five minutes the boy came over and asked her to dance. He was very good-looking and spoke fluent English. They threaded their way onto the dance floor. They made a handsome couple. Fleur was just admiring them and wondering why English people were so hopeless at foreign languages compared to the rest of the world, when she felt a brisk tap on her shoulder.

"You dance, please?" came a high, commanding voice in broken English.

Fleur turned to see a small, sandy-haired boy, whose earnest, freckly face made him look about twelve, standing before her in a rigid posture. For a moment she almost burst out laughing and racked her brains for some excuse. Not being able to think of one quickly enough, she got up reluctantly and was at one seized in a firm embrace and propelled backwards across the dance floor at reckless speed. Towering above the boy, she glanced back over his head at Tony as they passed on their second rapid circuit of the floor. He caught her eye and at once collapsed forward onto the table in a shaking heap. The look was a big mistake, because Fleur immediately felt the laughter rising in her own throat and before she could stop it, it burst from her in a choking snort. Their dancing came to an abrupt halt, causing a minor pile up on the floor as her partner struck her forcefully on the back. This had the effect of making the choking worse and almost sent her into convulsions. She had to be led, coughing and spluttering, back to the table. There the young man deposited her and, with a short bow and a Teutonic click of the heels to Mr Taylor, he disappeared into the crowd with obvious relief. It couldn't have been greater than the relief Fleur felt, and when at last she was able to speak, she gasped at Tony, "Thanks a lot! You nearly made me choke to death back there."

"I'm sorry, but you can't imagine what you looked like!" He fell into another seizure of laughter and when the fit had finally subsided, Fleur announced that she had had quite enough dancing for one night and would be happy just to sit back and observe the scene. Mr Taylor ordered another bottle of wine and the rest of the evening passed pleasantly with Fleur politely refusing the few offers she got, none of them from local boys, and giggling with Tony. Jan hadn't been seen for a couple of hours, and when at last she did return to their table, Fleur could tell from her bright eyes and moony face that she was in love. She sighed inwardly, bracing herself for a sleepless night listening to Jan go on about what Fritz, or whatever his name was, had said and done in every detail.

THE NEXT MORNING she could hardly believe that she'd even had time to drop off, when Jan woke her by flinging open the shutters and declaring in a joyful voice, "God, it's a lovely day. Time to get up and enjoy it, sluggabed!"

Fleur groaned and buried her face in the pillow, away from the sudden intrusion of blinding light.

"Tell you what, I'll go and make the breakfast and bring it in so that you can have yours in bed," Jan said kindly, and bounced off to the kitchen.

Moments later she was back with a tray, beautifully laid out with coffee, fresh bread, butter and apricot jam. It was impossible to ignore such a nice gesture, so Fleur forced herself to sit up, bleary eyed and irritable, to receive the tray across her knees. "Thanks," she muttered.

Jan laughed affectionately. "If only you could see yourself! You look like Shock Headed Peter."

Fleur put up her hand to feel her tousled locks. They were stiff with salt and standing on end. She didn't need Jan to remind her of the sight she made.

"Thanks," she repeated in a surly tone.

"I'm sorry. I didn't mean to be horrid. In fact you look rather sweet."

"Oh, better and better!"

"All right, not sweet. But anyway, let me tell you about my plan for today."

Fleur groaned.

"Listen, you'll like it. Kurt's going to the beach with some friends for a late lunch picnic, and he asked if we'd come along."

"We? He doesn't even know me."

"He does, by sight. Anyway I've told him about you and he'd like to meet you. There'll be some friends of his."

"Oh I see. Someone for me, you mean."

"Well, you never know. I mean, you might like them, and what else are we going to do?"

"Oh, all right. Only don't try and get me off with someone, that's all. Just act like I'm not there."

"That'll be the day! This isn't my friend, it's the flagpole!"

Fleur laughed despite herself. It was impossible to resist Jan's good humour.

At two o'clock, after elaborate preparations, they were ready to set off. As they emerged from the shady courtyard into the glare of the street, Fleur noticed a Corsican boy leaning against the wall of a house opposite. He appeared to be watching them. She had already caught sight of him a couple of times before from the window of their flat, not always in the same place, but always seeming to be focussed on their house. He was attractive, not very tall, like most Corsicans, but quite strongly built with dark hair that curled slightly over the collar of his clean white shirt. There was something strange about him, a sort of stillness. He did not look at them as they passed but went on leaning against the wall and staring straight ahead of him.

When they had gone a few yards down the street, Fleur said to Jan, "Did you notice that boy standing opposite our house?"

"No. What about him?"

"Oh, nothing. I think I've seen him before, that's all."

"He probably lives near by."

"Yes, perhaps."

But the explanation didn't satisfy Fleur and she continued to wonder about the boy as they made their way to the beach.

The beach was very hot and fairly empty because the hotel dwellers had gone back for their lunch and siestas. Kurt and his friends had already established their position and were lying on raffia mats under brightly coloured umbrellas. The sounds of David Bowie reverberated at a discreet volume from their tape recorder and there was a picnic of cold meats, bread and fruit laid out on a white cloth. There were also glasses, a couple bottles of white win in a ice bucket and some bottles of Perrier. Kurt got up and came to meet them. His body was bronzed and athletic and his mirror sunglasses completed his look of casual sophistication. He kissed Jan on both cheeks and held out his hand to Fleur as Jan introduced them. Then he led them back to the group, holding Jan by the hand. Fleur was already wishing she hadn't come.

"This is Elsa, Elena, Volker, Mitzi, Helmut and Andrea." He indicated six tanned, lean bodies reclining on their mats, who shifted slightly to say a languid hallo. Fleur nodded at them, instantly forgetting their names.

"Help yourself to food, please," Kurt said.

One of the boys, Volker, who was lying next to the ice box, picked up a bottle of wine and waved it in their direction. "A drink? Wine or Perrier?" he asked in English.

"Wine, please," Jan said. "Well, this is nice. Quite a feast!"

Volker smiled.

"You like chicken?" he said, indicating the delicate slices of pale meat in melting aspic that lay in a plastic container. "You help yourself, please."

"Thanks, it looks delicious," Jan said, taking a paper plate and serving herself generously.

"You too?" Volker said turning to Fleur. Then he added with a sly smile, "Or are you too 'chicken' already?"

Mitzi and Andrea giggled and Helmut made a clucking noise from his reclining position then dissolved into quiet conspiratorial laughter. Andrea buried her face in his naked, bronzed side. Fleur smiled weakly. She had no idea what was going on. She supposed that Volker had made a joke but she felt very uncomfortable.

"No, thanks. I'll just have some bread and fruit, if I may," she said.

She declined the wine in favour of Perrier, feeling that

she needed to keep her head, took her plate and went and sat down on the far side of Jan. Jan had already taken off her dress, spread out her towel and sat down under Kurt's umbrella.

"The sun, she is hot today. Good for the browning," Volker said conversationally.

"Yes, almost too hot," Fleur said, covering herself liberally with sunscreen.

"You accustom yourself soon, I think."

"Oh, yes. I expect so. How long have you been here?"

"Three weeks. In another week we return to Germany. I am sad."

"Yes. I expect I'll miss it when the time comes," she said.

She could think of nothing further to say.

Assuming the conversation was at an end, he lay back down on his mat and closed his eyes. One of the girls leaned over and tickled him lazily behind the ear. He laughed, and flung an arm around her. They lay with their noses almost touching, whispering and laughing. Fleur applied herself to the bread and fruit, wishing that she found it easier to talk to people. The Bowie tape came to an end and someone reached out and exchanged it for Janis Joplin. The sun felt blisteringly hot on Fleur's back. If she lay like this for long, she'd be burnt to a crisp. She glanced over at Jan, who had now moved closer to Kurt and was also engaged in whispered conversation, interspersed with the occasional coy giggle and slap. She was behaving in the way she had always despised the girls at school for, Fleur thought. In any case she certainly couldn't intrude on the two of them by asking if they would mind her sharing their umbrella. She decided to go for a swim.

The waves felt cold at first and she lifted one foot then the other at the water's edge, trying to accustom herself to the shock. But very soon she was in, floating on her back in the limpid water, staring up through half-closed lids at the brilliance of the almost colourless sky. On her way back from the sea, she met Kurt and Jan going down to bathe. Jan smiled at her in a trance of happiness and wiggled her fingers in a gesture of greeting. Fleur sat down on her towel again, hugging her knees to her chest and watching their small prancing forms dancing up and down in a halo of light and spray. They moved together and held one another in a distant embrace, his gleaming head bent down to her dark one, the sea glinting and sparkling around them. It was like something out of a movie and Fleur couldn't help feeling envious, however much she didn't begrudge Jan her happiness. She turned to the sleek forms of the Germans, who all seemed to have fallen asleep. She felt very lonely, cut off from them by their inscrutable air of sophistication even more than by the language barrier. She got out the book she'd brought with her and tried to read, but it was no good. She felt bored and out of place. She might as well pack up and go. She put on her dress, gathered her things into her beach bag and stood up.

"D'you mind telling Jan I've gone back to the flat? I think I've had all the sun I can take for today," she said to Volker's sleeping form.

He opened one eye drowsily. "OK. Good you could make it. See you around."

"Yes. Thanks. See you."

She turned away and trudged back along the beach. She climbed the steps onto the quay with a sense of relief. Now that she was actually alone, she felt less lonely. Some fishermen were mending their nets and watched her silently as she passed. In a little street that led away from the sea, two black clad women sat outside their houses on hard upright chairs, sewing, talking, and watching the children that played around their feet. Fleur smiled at them but got no response. The women only gazed at her blankly. She felt herself to be in some way intruding on them and hurried on up the street.

A little further on, she rounded a corner and came suddenly upon the church. Usually she'd only seen it from a distance, towering over the surrounding rooftops. She decided to go in and take a look. She pushed open the heavy door and then an inner door lined with green baize. A dank coolness greeted her, mingled with the scent of incense, and through the greenish, underwater light, she made out the long, squat nave leading to the high altar. Opening out from the nave were small side chapels, once painted a sort of pink but peeling now and green with damp. Above the altars hung pictures of saints with bloody wounds and eyeballs lolling heavenwards in an ecstasy of suffering, or was it joy? Either way it disturbed and slightly horrified Fleur. But the thing that she found entirely beautiful was the tower of glittering candles near the main altar, lovely as a Christmas tree. She walked towards it. An old woman was in the act of placing a fresh candle on a spike and lighting it. She saw Fleur and for a moment seemed about to give a greeting. Instead she made a harsh guttural sound in her throat and turned angrily away. Feeling very uncomfortable, Fleur walked back down the central aisle, puzzled by the woman's response to her. Then she remembered Jan's mother's warning about how much stricter the customs were in Catholic countries and that you shouldn't go into their churches with your head uncovered. How could she be so stupid as to have forgotten? She made for the entrance.

She was just pushing open the green baize door, when there was a rustling sound behind her. Claw-like fingers seized her bare arm, pinching it painfully, and a high, bird-like voice rapped out a torrent of irate words. Fleur turned in astonishment to see a tiny, wrinkled crone glaring angrily up at her. She wrenched herself free of the old woman's grip and pushed her way out into the sunny street.

What the hell was all that about? She inspected her arm and saw to her rage four half-moons where the old woman's nails had dug into her flesh. She turned and started to walk away from the church as quickly as she could. Disapproval was one thing but that was a vicious, unprovoked attack. *I didn't do anything to justify it. It wasn't as if I'd stepped too near the altar, or spat, or done something truly disrespectful. The only thing she could accuse me of was being improperly dressed. But what am I supposed to do? Shroud myself from top to toe in black like they do? Never be seen in public or dance at the disco or have any fun like the Corsican girls? This is the eighties, after all. They ought to be prepared to live and let live. After all, they're keen enough to take the tourists' money, however much they disapprove of them.*

As she reached a more familiar part of town and saw

the main square ahead of her, she began to calm down and slowed her pace. She had to admit that in their eyes she might have made a rather outrageous sight, with her bright dress, wild hair, naked limbs, in the quiet sanctity of their church. *I suppose it's not surprising they were a bit shocked really, narrow minded as they are. Well, I won't do it again.*

The shops were just beginning to reopen after the long siesta and there were renewed signs of life coming from the houses; radios playing, crockery chinking, the sounds of children and raised voices. But the tourists hadn't emerged yet and the streets around the square were almost deserted. As she entered the main square, Fleur's glance took in a group of local boys standing on the far side around some beat-up motorbikes. A couple of them she thought she recognised from the disco. Then she saw the boy who had been standing outside their house. He was one of the few wearing the more traditional cord trousers instead of jeans. She was surprised to see him laughing and chatting with others. She'd thought of him as rather a loner.

She had no very definite idea of where she was heading but wherever it was, by now unless she turned back and retraced her steps, she had to pass by the group of boys. They had seen her and were watching her approach. She braced herself for the inevitable catcalls and remarks and, looking firmly ahead of her, walked smartly on. She wasn't going to give them so much as a glance.

There were no whistles or catcalls but for the second time that afternoon Fleur felt horribly aware of her scantily clad body. She made a mental resolution to carry a cardigan about with her in future, however hot it was. When she was almost past the boys, she heard a whispered comment and smothered laughter, but a moment later she had turned the corner into an unfamiliar street and they were out of sight.

She slowed her pace and breathed more easily. *It was quite simple after all. They get the message pretty quickly if you keep your cool and don't encourage them.* The street she was walking down had a slightly different appearance from the ones she'd been in hitherto. The houses were more dilapidated and there were piles of rubbish which looked as if they'd become part of the landscape. The few children playing in the street were darker than Corsicans. Gipsies, or Arabs perhaps. On the wall of a small shop, three posters had been stuck up, one above the other. They showed a man in cord trousers and black beret, waving a rifle above his head, and there was some writing scrawled on the wall beneath — *Francesi Fora! Pinsuti Fora!* Fleur had no idea what it meant, but she knew that the man on the poster was Corsican and she remembered Jan's parents talking about the Corsican Nationalist Movement. This was probably something to do with it. Evidently, they wanted independence from France and didn't care how they got it. It seemed that virtually everyone was involved in it one way or another. It was organised into cells, whose headquarters were scattered through the mountains and were separate from one another to prevent betrayal. It sounded rather exciting to Fleur, like some old secret society, even though she was aware that it was capable of terrible brutality to those it considered its enemies.

A whine of Arab music started up from one of the houses. The children stared at Fleur with blank faces but there was nothing alarming about them. Then, from behind her in the direction of the square, there came the burst of motorbike engines firing up, an explosion of noise that settled down into a steady purr. They were on the move and Fleur had the sinking feeling that she knew where they were heading.

She moved over to the side of the street, walking near the wall. That way there would be plenty of space when they went roaring past her in a manly show of speed. But to her surprise the quiet throb of their engines scarcely increased, except that it was gradually coming nearer. She walked on, not quickening her pace or looking back. Ahead, the dirty street stretched endlessly, like a lesson in perspective. There wasn't a room for two cars to pass, and if one had come at her in the narrow gully she would have had to throw herself across its bonnet to avoid being crushed. She could hear their engines closer now. The hairs at the back of her neck began to prickle as she waited for them to catch up with her. Closer and closer they came — they would soon be at her heels. It was like a dream she had of running and running down a dark alley and never seeming to get anywhere, as her pursuers relentlessly closed in on her with the speed and silence of big cats. Her heart was bursting in her chest and her ears were pounding. They were right behind her now though she didn't turn her head. She felt as if she could almost hear them breathing. They kept pace with her exactly.

With mounting panic she forced herself not to break into a run. Then suddenly she knew what to do. She stopped dead in her tracks, turned and faced them. Eight bikes swerved and collided in a frantic effort to avoid her. Two of the riders turned too sharply and fell off. The others managed to keep their balance but circle perilously. They looked ridiculous in their confusion. Fleur felt almost light-headed with relief and triumph. She caught the eye of one of them and for a moment he stared back coldly. Then they wheeled round and roared off down the street, revving furiously. The two who had fallen off righted their bikes without looking at her, kicked their engines back to life, and scrambled off in pursuit of their mates. The walls of the little street shook with the echo of their thundering noise and they disappeared from sight.

Fleur leaned against the wall, feeling the strength go from her legs as if they were about to collapse beneath her. She felt dizzy and suddenly exhausted. With a great effort she stood away from the wall and began to retrace her steps. Some dark men came out onto the street. They stared at her but she no longer cared. She was sick of the lot of them. She walked on mechanically, towards the familiarity of the square. The cafés were just beginning to fill up after the afternoon lull. She saw it all without interest. What did these bronzed, carefree tourists know about the real life of this place? They went around, happily spending their money, with no idea of the savage resentment they caused. She saw it now and it depressed her infinitely. The only thing she wanted was to get back and collapse in the peace and sanctity of their flat.

As she passed the spot in the square where the bikers

had stood, she saw that the boy from outside their house was still there, chatting to a friend. It occurred to her that he couldn't therefore have been with the riders who'd come after her. The thought was unexpectedly comforting.

4

ENCOUNTER ON THE BEACH

The following morning Fleur slept late. When she awoke the flat was silent. A brilliant wedge of sunlight striped the floor beside her bed from the half open shutter. She got up. The tiles felt warm beneath her feet. She yawned and stretched and scratched her head, wondering what time it was and where everyone had gone to. She wandered into the kitchen. The clock said eleven. She must have slept for nearly twelve hours. No wonder she felt refreshed.

On the kitchen table there was a note propped against the sugar box. Fleur picked it up and read, "Coffee on the stove. Thought we'd better leave you as you were fast asleep. Gone into town. See you back here two o'clock lunch. Jan."

Fleur poured herself some coffee, cut a slice of bread, and sat down to her breakfast. The prospect of a morning to herself was quite pleasing. She took a cube of sugar out of the box and dunked it in her coffee, watching it turn brown, then popped it into her mouth just before it disintegrated. She spread her bread with jam and dunked that too. The jam spread out rosily into the brown liquid and when she ate the soggy morsel, it had a coffeeish taste mingled with the tang of fruit. This was the life! She began to think about what she was going to do for the rest of the morning. She couldn't be bothered to bath; besides, bathing in the sea every day meant that she was perfectly clean even if a little salty. In fact a swim was what she most felt like. The sea would be warm and the beach not too crowded at this time of the day since a lot of people didn't get there till after lunch. She would go straight there avoiding the town. The memory of yesterday's ordeal was now fairly remote but for the time being at least, she felt it wiser not to go walking round town on her own.

When she had finished her breakfast, she dressed, shoved her bathing things, comb, suntan oil and a book into her bag, found her watch and, full of high spirits, jogged downstairs to the courtyard. As she opened the door onto the street, she looked round for the Corsican boy, half-expecting to see him standing against the opposite wall. He wasn't there. She closed the door behind her and glanced up and down the street; only some women laden with shopping on their way home to cook the midday meal, a few kids playing, and a couple of old men on a bench in the square, deep in conversation. She felt disappointed. If she had come out alone and he was there, he might have spoken to her or made some sort of sign. She had the feeling that he was waiting for her. Whenever she saw him, he seemed to be looking at her in particular, even though their eyes never met. She had noticed him and thought how nice he looked when Jan hadn't even seen him and had no idea who she was talking about when she'd mentioned him. Perhaps he'd first noticed *her* because of her colouring, so different not only from the Corsicans but also from the majority of the tourists. He might well be looking for an opportunity to speak to her.

Corsican boys, she knew, were strictly brought up by their parents. They wouldn't just come up to a strange girl and start talking to her. It would take time and watching and the right opportunities to get into conversation. On the rare occasions she'd seen them with their own girls, who were always accompanied by their mothers or some other elderly female, they had pursued them cautiously, looking away and pretending to be occupied with something else whenever the older women had looked at them. *Rather like a stalking game — and suited to their more passionate natures, maybe. Can't imagine Jim Forbes bothering with anything like that.* Of course, it was different when they didn't respect or felt hostile to a person, as she'd found out only too well the previous day. But this boy hadn't been part of that group who'd come after her, and that meant he must have deliberately chosen not to be.

When she reached the beach, the sands near the town steps were crowded but, as she walked further along, they soon thinned out until the beach was almost empty. Fleur picked her way round children and dogs rummaging busily in the sand, stepping over prone bodies burned brown or lobster pink in the sun, and families equipped with entire suites of furniture in striped canvas. As soon as she had left them all behind, she stopped, spread out her towel and sat down. Behind her, the houses of the town rose in a steep curve of tangled streets and baked, earth-coloured roof-tops. At the far end of the beach the mountains, their outline softened in a milky haze of heat, curved down in a great blue horseshoe to enfold the winking brilliance of the bay. Above the glittering water the sky was not yet drained of colour and on the horizon where sky met sea, there were a few shreds of cloud. A slight breeze relieved the almost oppressive heat, stirring on the skin, soft as silk.

A wave of incredible happiness rose up in Fleur, a physical sensation experienced as a rushing burst of energy in the chest and throat. At that moment she felt completely happy. There was nothing else she wanted in the world but to be sitting there on that hot beach, surrounded by those blue mountains and that sparkling sea. She had only ever experienced such intense happiness before when she was in Wales. She pulled her dress off over her head and lay back, eyes half-closed against the glare, drinking in the heat and feeling the fine grains slip through her fingers as she gently kneaded the sand. She felt like singing but couldn't think of anything appropriate and besides someone might be listening. In a little while she sat up again, too full of happiness just to go on lying there. Perhaps she would go for a swim.

As she was making up her mind to get up and go down to the water, her eye was suddenly caught by a figure sitting on a rock at the far end of the beach where the hills met the shore. The figure was motionless, a black silhouette against the blinding light. She shaded her eyes with her hand to try to make it out more clearly. She could make out no details but something told her that it was the boy from the square.

She lay back again on the hot sand, her heart beating fast. It was ridiculous to get so worked up when it could be anybody. But she closed her eyes and strained her ears, listening for the least sound of someone approaching. She waited. For a long time she heard nothing, except the continuous rustle of sand grains shifting against one another in ceaseless activity beneath her, and far away the dim thud of waves breaking on the distant shoreline. Then at last there was a heavier vibration and the rhythmic squeaking of an approaching tread. A shadow passed over her face and was gone. The footsteps ceased. She opened her eyes a fraction, feeling that whoever it was must surely be able to hear her heart thumping. He was squatting on his haunches a few feet away from her and gazing out to sea. His smooth skin glowed dark against the white of his shirt and his hair gleamed in the sun with coppery lights, curling slightly over his tanned neck. His boots lay at his side, tied together by the laces. He did not move, though there was an air of slumbering energy about him as if he might jump up and race off at any minute. She felt she mustn't startle him, almost as if he were some sort of wild creature.

She pulled herself slowly up onto her elbows, trying not to grin from sheer nervousness. He turned and looked at her. His eyes, she noticed, had that liquid, unfathomable look that brown eyes sometimes have. Then, to her utter astonishment, he said in English, "My name is Paulo. What is yours?"

For a moment she was too surprised to speak. She had

never imagined that he would speak English, nor had it occurred to her how, if ever they did encounter one another, they were going to communicate.

He saw the astonishment on her face and grinned at her.

"My name's Fleur," she said.

"A French name. But you are not French?"

"No, I'm English."

She smiled back at him, glad that the ice had been broken between them so quickly.

"Wherever did you learn to speak English?"

He frowned slightly and said in a more formal tone, "I learn at school. They teach us something, even in Corsica."

She realised that she'd offended him, though quite without intention. She must be more careful.

"I'm sorry. That sounded rather rude. What I meant was, you speak such good English. I know hardly any French."

His face relaxed. "I get first prize in English," he said proudly.

"Did you? That's terrific!"

A silence descended and Fleur racked her brains for something else to say that would keep him there. But he didn't appear to find the silence at all awkward. He squatted on his haunches, idly poking at an insect hole with a bit of stick.

Eventually he said, without looking up, "You like it here?"

"Yes, I like it very much."

"It is best in spring. Not so much people."

"No. I bet it's lovely then. Before the tourists come."

"It is not so hot and there are flowers on the trees and in the mountains."

"I should like to see that. Do you live in the town?"

"No. Further up the island. In the mountains."

He glanced up at her, suddenly catching her full in the eye with his deep brown gaze so that she blushed to the roots of her hair.

"You like to take a walk? A little way, to the hills there?" He pointed to where the hills came down to meet the beach at the far end. "From there you see a long way."

Fleur considered for a moment. There seemed no harm in it and it was obvious from what she'd seen at the disco that there was no other way she was going to get to know him. There was plenty of time before lunch and Paulo was just the person to show her around.

"OK. Just a little way."

He stood up and offered his hand to help her to her feet. She took it, letting it go again as soon as she was upright. His touch startled her. His skin felt warm and slightly rough to the touch, and he smelt of new mown hay with a faint sea smell. She stood close to him for a moment, unable to look at him, uncertain what to do next. Then she stepped back, picked up her dress, put it on and stuffed her things into her beach bag.

"Ready," she said.

Paulo set off, walking with long, easy strides, his boots thrown over one shoulder. He wasn't walking fast but he seemed to cover a lot of ground quickly and sometimes she had to run a step to keep up with him. Once or twice he paused to wait for her. As they went she stole glances at his profile. He had a fine, rather aquiline nose, the sort of profile that might be called noble rather than handsome. In fact there was something rather noble about him, Byronic almost. She was beginning to relish the slight sense of risk she felt at trusting herself to this total stranger. It was exciting, an adventure.

As they neared the end of the beach, she noticed that the clouds had begun to gather. They were no longer shreds on the horizon but building up over the hills, blowing in from the sea.

"Look at that! Surely it's not going to rain?" she said.

He frowned slightly. "Perhaps. It is early for rain, but sometimes we have storms in summer. I do not think it will rain yet."

He turned to her and smiled. His smiles came as much of a surprise as everything else about him. They almost took her breath away. It was impossible not to smile back. She was afraid she must keep grinning rather foolishly.

"What do you do when it rains?" she asked.

"We stay home," he said.

At the end of the beach a steep path led up between rocks. Paulo started up it, climbing rapidly between the stony clefts despite his bare feet. Fleur followed more slowly, hanging on to rocks and bushes grazing her knees and panting for breath. At the top he was waiting for her. She gasped at the view. The ground had flattened out into a huge plateau sloping upwards to green foothills and, higher still, dark mountains bare of foliage. Woods edged the stretch of dry, yellowish grass and scrub on which they now stood and below, to the left, the sea gleamed in an increasingly metallic light.

"It's beautiful!" she said.

They gazed ahead of them, each absorbed in their own thoughts.

"We go a little further?" he said, turning to her. "From that hill there you see all the bay."

He was pointing to one of the nearer foothills. She hesitated. It wasn't far but it was a long way from the beach and she wondered for a moment whether she should be there at all with a perfect stranger. But Paulo didn't seem like a stranger. She felt quite at home with him.

"All right. But then I must go back. I'm expected home in time for lunch."

They walked on, covering the distance rapidly for space was deceptive in this wide, clear landscape. Over to the right was a small wood. There was a sudden flicker of lightning in the darkening sky behind it and an echoing roll of distant thunder though the clouds had not yet obscured the sun. From between the trees a swift, long-legged creature bounded and shot away across the uneven ground in high, zigzagging leaps.

"Whatever's that?" Fleur exclaimed, stopping in her tracks.

"A chamois. They live in the woods. We hunt them sometimes."

"How lovely! Not you hunting them, I don't mean," she added quickly. "It must have been startled by the thunder. We'd better be getting back."

Storms always excited rather than alarmed her but all the same, she thought, it was probably wiser not to get caught up here in one. There was nowhere to shelter.

"Only a little further," he said. "It will not rain yet."

He took her hand. His touch went through her like electricity. It left her feeling relaxed, quiescent. They were only a few minutes from the rise. She might as well go on now they had come so far. Hand in hand they walked on.

Keeping an eye out for chamois, she saw another movement in the edge of the trees. A figure emerged, not running or leaping but walking quite slowly. She realised with some surprise that it was a man and that he was holding a rifle in his hands.

"Who's that? A hunter?" She pointed at him.

"Perhaps. It is he who frightens the chamois," Paulo said.

"I hope he's not going to shoot it." She couldn't bear the thought of that delicate, leaping creature being felled by a bullet. "There must be other things to eat around here."

She glanced at Paulo. He was staring ahead, frowning slightly. When she looked ahead again, she saw that a second figure had emerged from the other side of the wood. He too carried a gun and she could see now that they had ammunition belts round their cord trousers. Jan's phrase went through her mind, "The Corsican Nationalist Uniform," and suddenly she began to be afraid. One of the men raised an arm and shouted. Out of the corner of her eye, she saw Paulo make an answering gesture with his free hand. The two men were walking towards them, their paths converging. Paulo's grip on her hand tightened, but it wasn't affection. She knew clearly now that it was because he wanted to hold on to her. He hadn't seemed at all surprised when the two men came out of the wood. And if they weren't chamois hunters, what *were* they after?

She wrenched her hand free from Paulo's grasp. He grabbed after her but missed and she started to run back in the direction they had come. She ran blindly with all her force, stumbling over scrub and stones but never quite losing her balance, driven on by the force of panic. She heard the men shouting behind her and heavy boots pounding and scraping on stones in quick pursuit. Her lungs were bursting in her chest. She knew that she could never get away from them but ran all the same in the frantic, automatic hope that she could save herself. There was the sound of a car revving over to the right and tyres spitting stones as it roared towards her over the rough ground. Out of the corner of her eye she saw it approaching to cut off her flight. But she could not stop. At any moment they would catch her but she would never, never give herself up.

Something struck her a blow at the back of the neck and she fell to the ground like a stunned rabbit, hitting her forehead on a stone. The last thought that went through her mind was, "My God, they've killed me!"

5

PRISONER

A rock rolled slowly towards the edge of the precipice that towered above her. Fleur saw it first as a great shadow that blotted out the sun. It spun in slow motion off the cliff top, rolling and turning in mid-air. She ran this way and that looking for cover, trying to escape its falling mass. Then it began to disintegrate, showering into a million little pieces like shrapnel or golden rain. There was no escape. Her head ached unbearably in anticipation of the coming blow. But before it fell, the dream began to fade. If she tried very hard she might be able to wrench open her eyelids, stop the nightmare. With a great effort she opened them half-way. She could see nothing except a dim, underwater light. But the headache went on. She closed her eyes again and lay very still, hoping that the pain would ease. Her whole body ached. Fragments of memory began to glimmer in the spaces between the throbbing pain. There was something she had to think about. But not yet, not yet. She lapsed back into sleep.

When she woke again she opened her eyes and saw a bare, dimly lit room with a shuttered window. A little, faded light seeped in from the shutters. It must be getting dark. Memory began to return. She had no idea where she was or how long she had been there, but she knew with sick clarity that she had been captured. She was a prisoner! The thought was so frightening that for a moment her mind seemed to slip its hold. She closed her eyes again, willing unconsciousness. But it would not come. There was no help for it, she was alive and awake and had to face whatever terrible things had happened to her.

She turned her head cautiously to the right, wary of the pain, so that she could get a better view of the room. It had a cobbled floor and there was no furniture except an upright wooden chair and a washstand with a jug and basin next to the bed she lay on. Someone had thrown what looked like an old coat over her. It felt chilly and there was an intermittent rumble of distant thunder. She remembered that there had been a storm but it sounded as if it had moved away. Slowly she began to turn over onto her side but as she did so a blinding pain shot through her temple. She tried to raise her hand to her head but discovered that her wrists had been tied. She lay back, sobbing as hard as her head would stand, filled with unbearable desolation.

The noise of her sobbing must have aroused her captors because the door opened and a big woman came into the room. She was dressed in black and carried a bowl in her hands. She came over to the bed and placed the bowl next to the basin on the washstand. She leaned towards Fleur, peering into her face.

"Leave me alone!" Fleur cried, shrinking in fear.

The woman said something harsh and incomprehensible in reply and angrily gestured for her to lie down again. She did so, watching the woman fearfully for what she would do next. She wasn't a young woman, probably in her fifties, dressed in the usual black of that generation, but she was strongly built and looked as if she'd stand little nonsense. *She could kill me if she wanted to, and there wouldn't be a thing I could do about it,* Fleur thought in horror.

The woman reached towards her. But instead of tightening the ropes that bound her as Fleur expected, she undid them. Fleur spread her fingers and rubbed her wrists which were chafed from the rope, keeping an eye on the woman, who lifted a rag from the basin on the washstand and squeezed it out. Reddish drops of water dripped from it as she did so. She leaned forward and wiped Fleur's forehead with the rag, moving it quite gently over the tender places. Fleur began to sob quietly. The woman spoke again in her deep, harsh voice in a language that wasn't French and sounded more like Italian. Fleur turned her face to the wall so that she couldn't see how afraid of her she was. The woman said no more but went and sat down on an upright chair on the other side of the room.

Fleur must have fallen asleep again, for when she next opened her eyes it was quite dark except for a candle burning in a saucer on the washstand. The big woman was still seated on the wooden chair. She was knitting and

Fleur could hear the steady click of her needles. Seeing Fleur stirring, she put down her knitting and came over to her. She reached down and lifted her as if she were a doll into a sitting position. At close quarters she smelt heavily of garlic with a faint tang of lavender. Fleur made no resistance. Let the woman do what she liked with her, she was too weak and afraid to resist. She must wait until she was better. Meanwhile, she must behave with the utmost quietness and cunning and, perhaps, if all her captors were no worse than this woman, she might just have a chance of survival.

The woman picked up the bowl from the washstand and brought it towards Fleur's lips. Fleur put down her head obediently and was about to drink, when such a goaty smell reached her nostrils that she turned away, retching. Another wave of despair overwhelmed her. They were trying to poison her! Well, she would not eat their disgusting food, not if she died of starvation. The woman replaced the bowl on the washstand with a tutting sound of annoyance, settled the pillow behind her so that she could sit a little more upright, and went out of the room. A moment or two later she returned with another bowl and again presented it to Fleur. She sniffed at it cautiously, not daring to refuse. This time it smelt good and, despite her misery, Fleur realised how hungry she was. It must be at least twenty-four hours since she'd last eaten. It was better to eat and build up her strength than to give up and die. She took a spoonful, under the watchful gaze of the woman. The hot liquid slipped down her throat, warming and reviving her. She began to feel a bit more hopeful. Judging from the woman's behaviour towards her so far, perhaps they weren't planning to kill her. Then they must want her for something else. Money? A ransom perhaps? From what she'd seen of these Corsicans they had little use for foreigners except money. No doubt they assumed the Taylors were rich. *The Taylors!* The thought flooded her with feelings almost too painful to be borne. She pushed them from her and forced herself to go on thinking. They would send them a ransom note, she reasoned, the money would be paid and then she would be set free. In fact the more she thought about it, the more likely that seemed.

She finished the soup and the woman carried the bowl out of the room, closing the door behind her. Fleur was left alone in the dim candlelight. Panic began to take hold of her once more. *What if the Taylors won't or can't pay up? Mum's got no money. Mum! Does she know yet? What's she doing? She'll be crazy with worry! Even if the money is paid will they let me go? Every day there are stories in the papers of hostages being shot to stop them from talking. Or the police advising relatives not to pay up and then finding them when it's too late. Will I ever get home?* She was overwhelmed by terror. It was all some appalling nightmare.

The following day she woke late after a restless night filled with frightening dreams. Her body felt bruised but less acutely painful and she felt calmer than the night before. She would have given a lot for a hot bath and a change of clothes but, from the primitive nature of the room she lay in, that seemed out of the question. She assumed she was in some sort of house. There was another room beyond her door, from which the smell of cooking reached her. But she heard no sounds of people other than the woman, no voices or comings and goings. Presumably they were alone together. The woman made a strange sort of jailer.

She swung her legs off the bed and stood up cautiously, taking care not to make any sudden movements because of her head. The headache had almost gone now but her head still felt tender and when she put her hand to her right temple, she could feel a long cut that was encrusted with dried blood. There was fresh water in the jug on the washstand. She poured some into the basin and gently washed her face and neck. Feeling refreshed, she looked round for something to dry herself with. Her eyes lighted on her beachbag in the corner of the room and again she was flooded with such an intense memory of the Taylors and their flat in the hot little town that for a moment she could hardly stand. She wrestled to blot out the memory, walked over to the bag, pulled out her towel and started to dry herself with deliberate concentration.

But it was not that easy to control her memories. She wandered round the room struggling to push them from her and wondering hopelessly what to do next. She went over to the window and opened the shutters a crack. An empty landscape greeted her, bare hills with a few scattered olive trees and not a house in sight. *My God, it's a desolate place!* she said to herself. *Where could I run to?* A dog barked in the distance. *A guard dog most likely. It could hunt me down in a couple of minutes. What if I got away but was caught and brought back? They'd punish me, and then I'd be even worse off than I am now, if that's possible. No, I'd better sit tight and wait and hope for the best. But what if I'm not found? How will I bear the waiting?* She sat down on the wooden chair and slumped forward until her forehead rested on her knees, arms hanging limply at her sides. She remained in that position until eventually her attention was aroused by the sound of movement from the room beyond the door. She raised her head and listened. The smell drifting in under the door made her realise she was very hungry. She went over to the door and opened it a chink.

The room she saw was indeed a kitchen. In front of her the woman stood before a big range, cooking. Fleur opened the door a little wider then drew back in fear. A man sat hunched at the table in his shirt sleeves. He was bent over his plate, shovelling food into his mouth with a hunk of bread. She wasn't sure but she thought she recognised him as one of the hunters who had captured her. At that moment he looked up and caught sight of her in the open doorway. He gave a harsh growl and stood up, shoving back his chair with a scraping noise. The woman turned rapidly and taking in Fleur's presence, said something in a commanding tone. The man sat down again, as if reluctantly, and with a scowl resumed his eating.

The woman beckoned Fleur into the room. Fleur stood there, frozen with fear. She repeated the gesture nodding vigorously. Fleur came forward slowly, keeping a wary eye on the man. The woman ladled some food from the pot on the range into a bowl and handed it to her, then motioned her to go and sit down at the table. Fleur dared not disobey, though the last thing she wanted was to go near that man. She carried her bowl to the corner of the table furthest from the man and sat down on a wooden bench. The man took no notice of her and went on eating noisily. Fleur took a mouthful of the stew. It tasted rather strong and gamey, but delicious. She began to eat in small, quiet mouthfuls, all the while stealing glances at the man, who ignored her presence. He was younger than Fleur had at first thought, thickset, with a face lined about the mouth and eyes and a strong growth of beard as if he hadn't shaved for several days. His hands were rough and calloused, the fingers stiff and clumsy as he handled the hunks of bread that he used to push the food into his mouth. He looked hard and he frightened her.

A few moments later there was a tramp of footsteps outside and the sound of boots scraping on the step. She waited nervously. The house door opened and two men entered, stooping slightly to pass under the lintel. Both carried rifles. They were younger than the man at the table and the youngest, Fleur realised with a shock that made her suddenly feel sick in the pit of her stomach, was Paulo. The elder man held a dead hare in his hand, which he carried over to the woman then came and sat down at the table. Paulo put down his rifle by the door and patted the head of a thin, brown dog, who sat down beside the rifle as if it knew better than to try coming any further into the room. Paulo came to the table and sat down too. Fleur stared hard into her plate, determined not to catch his eye or to acknowledge him in any way. She was filled with anger and hatred. All she could think of was that he had deliberately led her to believe that he liked her and wanted to be friends and it had been nothing but a charade, a trick. For a moment her hatred of him even made her forget her fear. Nobody spoke.

The woman brought food for the men, addressing

them briefly. The elder man said something in reply but Paulo merely nodded. The woman didn't join them at the table but ate by herself, standing up at the range. The atmosphere was tense and awkward, due at least in part, Fleur thought, to her own presence. She felt a brief, bitter triumph at her power, but it was shortlived. As soon as he had eaten, Paulo got up from the table, spoke a few words to the woman, whistled up his dog and left the house. Because she had studiously avoided looking at him, Fleur didn't know whether he had looked at her or tried to make contact with her. In any case she couldn't care less, she told herself. Now that he had gone she had the chance to study the other man. She watched him discreetly as he ate. He was better looking than the eldest man, his face smoother and less heavily jowled. His complexion, like Paulo's, was fairer, his eyes brown rather than black. She guessed they might be brothers. He could possibly have been called good-looking, except that she noticed he never quite looked anyone in the eye, not even his brothers, and he had a way of putting back his head and running his fingers through the hair that grew thickly from his forehead that suggested he thought rather a lot of himself. She hoped desperately that they would both soon follow Paulo out and she sat on, staring at her empty bowl and trying to draw as little attention to herself as possible. Once or twice she felt the younger man's eyes on her and longed to be invisible. She felt utterly exposed, like some sort of specimen pinned to a board for anyone's inspection.

At last the men finished eating and got up from the table. When they had left the house, Fleur heaved a silent sigh of relief. The woman didn't seem to her nearly so dangerous as they were. Fleur had even begun to look on her in a sort of way as her protector.

She spoke to Fleur now in a commanding tone. Fleur didn't understand a word she said but eventually she gathered from her gestures that she wanted her to collect up the dishes and clear the table.

Bloody cheek! You'll be lucky! she muttered under her breath. They weren't going to turn her into their skivvy on top of everything else! She was here totally under protest and the sooner they understood that and left her alone, the better.

She felt a stinging blow on the side of her head. It almost knocked her sideways and brought tears to her eyes. The woman repeated her command in a stronger voice and moved back to the range. Fleur got up, shaken and sullen, fighting to control her tears, and began to pile the bowls and plates together and to gather up the crusts of bread. She was seething with anger and hatred but she dared not disobey. The woman watched her from a distance but made no further move in her direction. As soon as she could, Fleur slunk off back to the haven of her room. It was a pretty depressing place but at least she felt safer there. It wasn't yet dark and she'd only been up for a few hours, but nevertheless she got back into bed and pulled the blanket up over her head to shut out the gloomy, partial light that seeped through the shutters, and willed sleep. At last she managed to drift off into a state that was half-sleeping, half-waking in which dream mingled with reality, numbing her awareness.

· · ·

THE NEXT DAY and the ones that followed she spent as much time asleep as possible, when she wasn't busy with the chores the woman gave her which took up most of the day. She was constantly brought face to face with the hardships of life here. Not just by the endless chores, but also by the lack of all comforts. For example, there was no bathroom and what washing she was able to do had to be carried out in cold water in a tin basin in her room. She began to note down details of her everyday life in a note-book she'd found, together with a felt tipped pen, in her beach bag. Writing them down made her feel that she was a little more in control of her existence, and soothed her in her worst moments by giving her something to do.

TODAY IS my 3rd day of captivity. Yesterday I managed secretly to break off a tiny piece of soap from the big lump in the kitchen without the woman noticing. A bit later I persuaded her to let me take some hot water from the copper on the range to wash my hair and clothes, which were filthy. I had to wash my clothes just before I went to bed, tipping the water away out of the window when I'd finished and hanging the clothes out to dry on the back of the chair and the bedrail because I've nothing else to wear. In the morning they were still damp when I came to put them on. I stood near the range whilst I ate my breakfast, shivering and steaming, hoping they'd dry quickly before I caught my death of cold. It gets quite chilly at night and in the early mornings up here in the mountains...

But the lavatory is the worst thing of all. It's in an outhouse, a wooden seat suspended over a stinking pit with the flies constantly buzzing round it. The first time I went there I thought I was going to be sick, and even now I never go until I'm forced to. I'm getting more used to it though — they say human beings can get used to anything! I take a deep breath just before I go in, then breath very lightly through my mouth. While I'm sitting there I cover my head with my arms to keep off the flies. That way it isn't nearly so bad. Of course there isn't any paper and I don't want to use up too many pages of my notebook.

Thursday (I think it is, though it's hard to keep track of the days here). Every morning when I get up, the men have already left the house, which is a relief. The woman gives me breakfast of goat's milk, which I've got used to now, and little fried cakes made out of chestnut flour: they are delicious. Then I spend most of the day helping the woman out with the chores, fetching water, scrubbing pots, cleaning and preparing vegetables for the evening meal, and other chores. I hate them but it's better than being idle, I suppose. It leaves me less time to think. The woman herself works like a donkey all day, milking and tending her goats, making their milk into cheese, peeling and pounding chestnuts into flour, cooking bread, soups and stews.

The job I hate most is peeling chestnuts. The sharp husks cover your fingers with a mass of little painful cuts and the fleshy part never wants to come away from the shell. It reminds me of Wales, of making the stuffing for the Christmas turkey. The first time I had to do it, I could hardly stop myself from sobbing out loud, I felt so terribly homesick. But I stopped myself because I don't want the woman to know how bad I feel and how frightened I am. If she thinks I'm bearing up all right, she may be inclined to treat me with more respect and leave me alone. After about half an hour, she saw that I hadn't even finished half the bowl of chestnuts and was very annoyed. She took the bowl from me, saying something in a cross voice which as usual I couldn't understand, and handed me a bowl of apricots to stone instead. I ate quite a few of them whilst she was outside working in her vegetable patch. Serve the mean old bag right! I could see her through the window with an old straw hat on her head, digging away in the stoney earth. She'll be lucky if she gets much to grow in that soil!

Friday. Today, my fifth, I have been allowed out for the first time. The woman let me help her in the vegetable garden this morning. Digging in that soil is backbreaking work but it's lovely to be out in the fresh air and see the sky. I looked round at the surrounding mountains and thought again that there's nowhere to run to, only empty space. Sometimes I can't believe any of this is really happening...

It's no good just feeling sorry for myself. I've got to try and survive somehow until I'm rescued. The best way is to distract myself from my troubles. So I'll start by describing the house. It isn't quite as primitive as I first thought, though it certainly lacks all mod cons. The main room is the kitchen, which is big, but the furniture is basic, just a table, a bench and four upright chairs, a wooden settle and a hard armchair by the fireplace, a chest and a sideboard. The sideboard is the one thing of relative luxury. It's covered with a lace cloth and framed photographs of stiffly posed people all in their black Sunday best, except for a baby, three young children and a bride, who wear white. Above the sideboard is a picture of the Virgin Mary and the baby Jesus, and above each doorway is a wooden cross with a dusty palm frond stuck in it. The family all seem to sleep in one room, though I haven't seen into it. I can imagine the crush though. I sleep in what must normally be the mother's room. I realised a while ago that the three men must be brothers and the woman their mother, but so far I haven't seen any sign of a father.

In the kitchen there are loads of cooking things, almost as many as in Jan's kitchen (but I can't afford to think of that). They're piled up all round the range and hanging on the walls of the alcove behind it. Food is obviously very important and we eat well. Sausages and smoked hams hang from the rafters between bunches of herbs. In one corner of the room there is a stack of wine kegs, one filled with olive oil. I love the colour of the oil, greenish gold, with a smell like tar as well as olives. I think they must press their own olives because one day I peered up into the loft when the mother was outside, and saw an ancient press up there with some olives still in it. You reach the loft by a flight of shallow, tiled steps from the kitchen. It forms the upper part of the house. The smell of ripe apples and melons comes down to the kitchen from the fruit that's stored in long rows on wooden racks.

On the other hand the family seem to think nothing of clothes. They only appear to own two sets of clothes each, one for ordinary wear, one for best. Once the two older brothers got dressed up to go out in the evening. They looked ridiculous, almost unrecognisable in dark, old-fashioned suits with their hair brushed flat, and they walked in a funny stiff way. It certainly didn't improve their appearance. Paulo only goes mooching out with his dog. He's quite a lot younger than the others and seems rather turned in on himself. But I'd rather not think about him.

In the evening after supper it's very quiet with no radio or TV. The mother mends or patches the men's clothes and sometimes she knits, on big needles with unbleached wool. The smell of the wool reminds me of the tufts I used to collect from the fences and hedgerows in Wales, and I get terrible bouts of homesickness. Sometimes I feel so desperate I think I may go mad.

Mum must be frantic with worry. And what about the Taylors? Have they got the ransom message yet? Are they managing to raise the money? I can't let myself think too much about any of this. Sometimes thoughts of my former life crowd in on me before I can stop them, especially pictures of Wales. I can see the courtyard of weedy slate flags in front of our farm and the children playing there with their broken-down bikes and little wooden horses John made, or Mum hanging out the flapping sheets to dry on a bright, gusty day, reaching up so that her blouse comes untucked from her skirt. I get a tight feeling in my chest and throat as if I'm about to suffocate. I shut my eyes tightly and start counting, breathing in and out deeply twice to each count. By the time I get to five the picture has usually begun to fade. But just occasionally these memories aren't so painful, in fact they can even be a bit of a comfort, reminding me of a time when I was happy and the possibility that one day I shall be happy again. Life in Wales was also pretty primitive, though not so bad as this.

TOWARDS THE END of this entry, the felt tip was beginning to run out. The next time Fleur tried writing with it, the pen had dried up completely. She threw it out of her bedroom window in disgust and despair. Now she had no outlet, nothing to confide her thoughts to. She was wholly dependent on her present environment, which gave her no opportunities of expressing herself. She couldn't even speak the same language as anyone else. Her only escape might be the novel she still had in her beach bag. But somehow she couldn't face that. Not just because reading seemed an odd thing to do in this household and she would have felt very conspicuous if she'd sat down by the fireside after supper with a book, but also because the story held no interest for her here. It had nothing to do with this life and the thought of it irritated rather than comforted her.

On her fifth day, shortly after the pen had run out, she was alone in the kitchen. It was the middle of the day and the mother was in one of the outhouses making cheese. Fleur had just gathered together a pile of vegetables to clean and chop for the soup, when Paulo came into the house. She was very surprised to see him. Normally the men never appeared during the day. He came straight towards her and she caught his serious, slightly anxious look before she had time to glance away. At the sight of him she suddenly felt like crying, tears of rage as much as misery. He was the only one who had any connection with her real life and she was still filled with anger at the way he had deceived her. The injustice of his betrayal was almost as hard to bear as the bouts of panic-filled home-sickness.

Paulo watched her, as he fidgeted nervously with the baby marrows that were waiting on the table to be chopped. Eventually he said, "I want you to understand, we do not hurt you. You have the word of my brothers and myself."

She looked up at him. He was very ill at ease. "Well, thanks a lot! I must say that makes me feel a whole lot better!"

"I am very sorry for what happened," he went on quietly.

She saw how much it cost him to speak but it did not

make her feel any less angry. "D'you really think that apologising can make it all right? D'you think I'll just say, 'Oh, fine, Paulo. Glad that's all cleared up.' You must be an idiot! Or so arrogant about your precious cause that you don't think anything else matters."

He flushed.

She saw with pleasure that she had wounded him. She would insult him in every way she could, especially when it was the truth she spoke.

"I know it is impossible you understand why we do this," he said.

"I'll say. I suppose it's for the money, though that seems to me a pretty pathetic reason for doing anything!"

He stiffened and drew himself more upright. "It is not just for the money," he said coldly. "It is for our Movement."

"Well, it's called kidnapping and terrorism where I come from. You're criminals!"

"Our Movement must have money. How else are we ever to free ourselves?"

"Oh, are you slaves, then? I'm afraid I hadn't noticed."

His face darkened with anger at her sarcastic tone. Suddenly, she felt afraid. She couldn't afford to alienate him totally. After all he was the only one who spoke English and the nearest thing to an interpreter that she had.

"And you don't care who you hurt in the process," she said, slightly less aggressively.

"For centuries we suffer. One invader follows another and always to conquer, steal and kill. Now it is the French. We will no longer live under a foreign power, to give our land and strength for others to grow rich while we grow poorer and weaker. The land is ours. The whole Corsican people feels this."

"But why *me?*" she almost shouted.

"Because you are a tourist and tourists are rich. We cannot make them listen to us in any other way."

The passionate conviction of his words stirred her to a grudging feeling of sympathy, even admiration for him. He believed so absolutely in what he said.

"Well, I'm sorry, but that doesn't make me feel any better," she said more quietly. "It's not even true!"

She began to cry, staring down into her lap in an effort to hide her tears. Whatever their justifications, their fight had nothing to do with her. She was merely an innocent bystander, an accidental victim whom they had stumbled upon, one who very well might get crushed to death in the encounter.

"I'm sorry," he muttered. "They pay the money soon, then you go free."

"*Who* will pay?" she cried, so frustrated she wanted to beat him with her fists.

But he turned on his heels and left the house.

"That's right! Turn your back and leave! Coward!" she sobbed. "You haven't even got the guts to face the result of your own actions!"

Why did he persist in seeing her as rich? If they had wanted someone who could pay the ransom, why hadn't they chosen one of the really rich tourists? They were almost all better off than she was, except that these stupid peasants were too ignorant to see it. She thought of her mother, sitting at home waiting for the telephone to ring, crazy with worry, and sobbed till her whole body shook. She did not hear the woman come into the room but felt a pair of strong arms go round her and her head cradled onto an ample bosom that smelt of garlic and lavender. She was in such need of comfort that she let it rest there, weeping until she was exhausted. When her sobs began to die down the woman led her to the bench, folded a jersey to make a pillow for her head and, laying her down, covered her shuddering body with a shawl. She stroked her hair, murmuring, "*Dors, Flora,*" and sat beside her until she saw that Fleur was at last quiet and had fallen asleep.

IN THE DAYS THAT FOLLOWED, despite her continuing mistrust and fear of the mother, Fleur grew to depend on her more and more as the one stable thing she could cling to. She was angry with Fleur whenever she saw her lazy or slapdash in her work, but she wasn't unjust and she didn't hit her again. She could be as severe with her sons if she considered them in the wrong. In fact it was this very severity that made Fleur believe that she would come to her defence if she saw her wrongly attacked, and that gave her what precarious sense of security she had in the household. She rarely saw Paulo now, and that was a relief. She was determined to avoid any further conversation with him. The feelings he aroused in her were too strong.

But Mama left her little time to sit and brood. Not only did she keep her busy all day long with the routine domestic tasks, which sent her to bed exhausted, but in the moments when her work was at last done, she tried to teach her things. For example, she taught her how to knit. She sat her down, put two knitting needles in her hand and showed her how to hold and twist the wool around the needles. At first Fleur was all fingers and thumbs. But Mama was very patient and slowly and painstakingly she began to get the hang of it. Bit by bit the stitches piled up until she had a visible piece of knitting about five rows deep. She inspected it with pride and satisfaction. Then, offended by a bit of loose thread that stuck out, spoiling the evenness of the pattern, she pulled at it and proceeded to unravel the whole lot. Mama watched her with a look of outraged disbelief. Then she threw back her head and roared with laughter. At first, Fleur was most offended by her reaction. Then she too began to laugh and they rocked back and forth with tears pouring down their faces.

She also tried to teach Fleur her language. Through pointing and sign language, Fleur began to learn the words for everyday things like bread, cheese, water, and simple phrases like "Clear the table," "Fetch some milk," and "Good girl." Gradually she and Mama were finding it easier to communicate with each other, at least on a practical level, and in turn that cut down the sources of friction between them. But as soon as the men came home, Fleur grew silent and afraid again. She never spoke for fear of drawing attention to herself; and she avoided their eyes, especially Paulo's, because he was the one who most often looked at her.

One evening at supper time the men had already sat down to eat, when Mama handed Fleur a dish of hot chestnut cakes to carry to the table. Jesu, the middle brother, had been watching her every movement out of the corner of his eye like a cat watching a bird while it pretends to be asleep. She had caught him watching her like this before, with a look that was both cruel and lazy at the same time, as if his contempt for her just outweighed his interest. She felt instinctively that he was the most dangerous of the three brothers, the only one who might start some terrible, tormenting game if ever they happened to be alone together.

As she passed by his chair, he suddenly shifted it and moved his foot. She tripped and fell headlong onto the floor, showering the cakes before her. He laughed unpleasantly. Ermano made an angry tutting noise, Paulo was silent. Fleur saw Mama's legs striding towards her as she grubbed about the floor trying to retrieve the broken cakes. She braced herself for the coming blow. But instead, the big woman bent heavily down beside her and helped her to gather up the bits. When they had finished, she got up painfully, banged the dish onto the table and said something in a harsh voice to Jesu. Fleur was sure that it was an order to leave her alone. He answered in a rough, surly tone, but his manner suggested that he knew he must submit to his mother, or at least go about it more subtly if he wished to torment her. The meal that followed was a tense, miserable affair. No one spoke and Fleur scarcely raised her eyes from her plate. As soon as it was over Paulo went out with his dog and when the dishes had been washed and put away, Fleur slipped off to her room.

It must have been about two weeks after her arrival, with day following day in routine work interrupted only by bouts of paralysing despair, that Fleur woke one morning sensing that it was later than usual. Mama hadn't called her and she could see from the angle of the light through the shutters that the sun was already high in the sky. She wondered anxiously what could have happened. Perhaps at last the ransom had been paid and she was going to be freed? She got up, put on her grubby dress and without bothering to wash or comb her hair, went to the door of her room and opened it cautiously. The kitchen was empty except for Ermano, who was sitting at the table in his shirt sleeves cleaning his gun. It was spread out in pieces all over the table. The breakfast dishes were stacked unwashed beside the range and a pot of stew was bubbling but there was no sign of Mama. Fleur felt suddenly weak with fear. Mama had never left her alone with any of the men before. Perhaps she was in the vegetable garden or out milking her goats? But there was a curious silence about the place which made her doubt it. Then where on earth could she have gone?

She walked across the room to the range, glancing out of the window as she did so for any sign of Mama. But there was none. She poured some hot water out of the copper into a basin and set about washing up as quietly as possible, taking care not to let the dishes chink against one another and so attract Ermano's attention. Perhaps if she saw her usefully occupied he would leave her alone. He ignored her and went on meticulously cleaning his gun. She strained her ears for the sound of footsteps that would herald Mama's return. But the minutes ticked by and there was no sound but the soft splash of water and the click and thud of metal against wood, as Ermano cleaned his gun and occasionally cleared his throat.

When she had finished the washing up, she looked round for another task in her feverish need to keep busy. She hadn't eaten any breakfast but even the thought of food choked her. What if Mama didn't come back at all? But that was ridiculous. She'd have to come back to her home. It couldn't be that the money had been paid because then Ermano would be out dealing with it, surely? Perhaps something had happened to Mama? Trickles of sweat ran down Fleur's spine and her forehead under her hair was damp from fear. She picked up a pile of chestnuts, sat down, and started to peel them mechanically. Their sharp skins hurt her less now that her hands were growing hard and callused from so much peeling and scouring. At long last she heard the sound of a dog barking, followed by voices and footsteps coming into the courtyard. Then the door opened and Mama came into the house.

Fleur stared at her in joy. She wanted to run over and fling her arms round her. But she sat still, knowing that such an impulsive gesture would not be appropriate. Besides, she wasn't alone. Behind her, as well as Paulo and Jesu, came two strange men. Mama took off her shawl and hung it on a peg near the door. Then she went to the sideboard, opened a drawer and carefully replaced her prayer book and rosary. *Of course*, Fleur thought, *it must be Sunday!* She had been to Mass. She knew that Mama was very pious. Every evening before bed, she knelt down in front of the Madonna and Child to say her Rosary. She had invited Fleur to join her on the first night, but had taken her reluctance as a sign that she held to a different faith and not pressed her, which Fleur had been grateful for. She had never been brought up to any religion and wouldn't have known what to do. She turned her attention now to the strangers. They were older than the brothers, dressed in dark Sunday suits and black berets. Their faces were weather-beaten and their hands, like Ermano's, were callused from work. But the respectful way in which everyone treated them made Fleur think they weren't just neighbours.

Mama fetched a bottle of wine and some glasses and placed them on the table, together with a plate of sliced salami and olives. Ermano cleared his gun to one side and all the men sat down together except for Paulo, who sat a little apart from them. Fleur noticed how his hand delicately stroked his dog's silky head and the quiet ecstasy with which she received his caress. Having served the men, Mama came over to Fleur at the range. She smiled at her conspiratorially and gave her shoulder a little nudge, before lifting the lid off the cooking pot to check the stew. She took no further part in the men's conversation and removed Fleur's bowl of peeled chestnuts from her, replacing it with some vegetables to peel and chop. She seemed concerned to keep her quietly occupied yet her manner to Fleur was unusually gentle. Fleur observed the strangers discreetly as she chopped.

One of the men was somewhat older than the other and it was he who did most of the talking. He spoke in short, rapid sentences in a rasping though not loud voice, as if accustomed to giving orders. Ermano and Jesu listened with attention. He sat in his chair, stiff and upright, and his bearing and manner had a military air which seemed at odds with his otherwise ordinary peasant appearance. The Movement, Fleur remembered, was like a secret, underground army, with cells like little regiments scattered throughout the mountains and a military discipline.

The chief ceased talking and Ermano said something. Then Jesu cut in with an angry tone. The chief turned on him and rapped out a command which at once reduced Jesu to silence, and after that neither of the brothers said anything for a while. It struck Fleur for the first time that Mama and her sons were nothing but small cogs in a much larger machine. New terrors crowded in on her. She was up against something far bigger and more frightening than just this family, whose prisoner she had thought she was. How would anyone rescue her in the face of all this organisation? The Movement was like a great octopus, whose tentacles reached out all through the mountains. Nothing escaped it! They might be planning to move her somewhere else, to people a lot worse than Mama. The Corsicans, she knew from Mr Taylor, had a violent history and were not afraid of using violence themselves. It had become almost second nature to them. But they had their code of honour all the same. Whatever the rest were like, she was sure that Mama and her sons would honour their agreement if the ransom was paid, and let her go unharmed. She clung fast to that belief because it was the only hope she had.

The men talked on and on. It seemed as if the two strangers would never leave. Fleur's empty belly was rumbling. She was sure the men must hear it across the room. But at last they got up to take their leave. The leader shook hands with Ermano and Jesu, then turned to bid Mama goodbye. As he did so his eye fell full on Fleur. It was the first time he had looked at her and his look chilled her to the bone. It was an expression of such cold indifference that it denied her very existence. She might have been an insect or a fossil in a glass case, rather than a fellow human being. His look told her that she bore as much relation to him, as the fossil did to the fishy creature that once swam the sea. All her courage failed her and she dropped her glance, feeling the sweat of fear break out on her body. When she looked up again the strangers were gone.

For the rest of the day everyone was very quiet. They ate their midday meal almost in silence. After it Ermano went back to cleaning the rifles, Jesu whittled at a candlestick he was making then went to sleep, and Paulo went out with his dog, returning at evening with a rabbit. Mama mended and knitted and Fleur was content to sit by her, needing the sense of security it gave her. She was especially gentle to Fleur and once she touched her cheek with her worn fingers. It was a gesture she had only ever seen her make to Paulo who, Fleur guessed from her face whenever she looked at him, was her favourite child.

After supper Fleur was sitting by the fire struggling with her knitting, when Paulo came over and stood beside her. She tensed.

"What do you make?" he asked.

"It's supposed to be a jumper. Eventually."

She grimaced, ashamed of how clumsy her efforts

must appear to him compared to his mother's skilled hands.

"You make a present?"

She heard the playful note in his voice.

"I doubt it'll be fit to give away. Anyway, I don't expect I'll have time to finish it," she said crossly.

"Then you take it with you when you go, and enough wool to finish."

She did not look at him but said, "No, thanks."

He walked away and sat down on the other side of the fireplace. He took a knife and piece of wood he'd been carving out of his pocket, and settled down to work on it. Fleur resumed her knitting, trying to ignore his presence. In a little while Mama brought her knitting over and came to sit near them. Ermano and Jesu had gone out so there were only the three of them, sitting together in the flickering firelight. It occurred to Fleur what a peaceful little group they would make to an outsider, each one absorbed in their work. *What a farce! Little do they know!* she thought, bitterly. She looked across at Paulo, his silky head bent over the piece of wood he was carefully carving. She could kick herself for being so foolish as ever to think that he was interested in her as a person. Seeing him there, so absorbed in his work, she hated him, and her longing at times for his friendship only increased her anger against him. Once she had trusted him. Now she knew that she must not let herself trust any of them, not even Mama. The visit of the two strangers had been a timely reminder that she must be on her guard all the time, that she could not afford the least feeling of hope or security.

There was no sound in the room, except for the logs

shifting and flaring in the fireplace, the click of knitting needles, and the faint scrape and chip of Paulo's knife against wood. Then, softly, Mama started to sing. She began in a low hum that was at once harsh and incredibly melodious. Her voice was strong but thin like an oboe, deep and unfemale but not male. *A sound which only people who live in high, lonely places would make, soft but carrying, sad and joyful at the same time.* Fleur had never heard anything like it. She let her hands fall idle in her lap. The voice seemed to surround her and enter into her like a lapping wave that calmed her anger and soothed her pain. She forgot where she was as if mesmerised. Slowly her eyelids dropped, a heaviness grew along her limbs and she began to drift into a relaxation so complete that it was more like a trance then sleep.

6

THE POWER OF MUSIC

The days passed and Fleur had heard no news of the outside world. Some days she waited, minute by minute, expecting at any moment that a message would come saying that the money had been paid and giving instructions about how and where she was to be returned to civilisation. At other times she almost forgot that it existed, so preoccupied was she by the dreary rhythms of her new life. She had grown used to the hard labour and lack of comfort. Feeling grubby and unkempt scarcely bothered her any longer. Her one dress grew increasingly shabby and colourless from frequent washing in cold water, and her hair was dry and wiry from being washed in soap. During the day she wore a dark apron that was much too big for her over her dress, and Mama had given her a jumper for when it was chilly. Fleur suspected that she had knitted it for Paulo. It made her arms and neck itch but it was warm and she loved its slightly sheepy smell.

She had come to accept her life here in a way, like being ill in hospital and knowing that it will end, though for the time being that was impossible to imagine. But the thing that still got her was the loneliness. However well she and Mama could now communicate about practical things, they couldn't really talk to one another. She had nothing to write with any longer, and she missed dreadfully having anyone of her own age around. She rarely saw Paulo except at meal times. Often she felt as if she had dropped out of the real world as surely as if she had died, that she would never see any of the people she loved again; just as if she had been erased from the face of the earth. The thought of school or London was like remembering a film she'd seen a long time ago. She could picture both quite clearly but they were unreal, as if they no longer had anything to do with her. She felt grief and longing only for her mother and their shabby flat and some of the ordinary things she shared with Jan, like the walk home from school each day. And now that she was no longer in continuous fear for her life, this longing grew stronger and more difficult to control. Sometimes, if she was alone, she would burst into a storm of weeping that left her exhausted, too tired to think any more. But when she was with Mama and the brothers, she retreated into a sort of numbness that she drew round herself like a cocoon. Mama sensed these moods and treated her gently, finding little tasks that distracted her but didn't require much concentration. But Mama's thoughtfulness only made it harder because it broke down her resistance, penetrating her anger and protective shell. Sometimes Fleur wished Mama was as callous and unfeeling as she had at first thought her, because then she could simply have hated her. As it was, she felt a painful confusion of conflicting feelings that swung back and forth from fear and hatred to something very like affection.

One morning she was in the kitchen scouring the big milk pan, when Paulo appeared. Mama was in the outhouse making goat cheese and Fleur was taken by surprise to see him at this hour of the day. They had hardly spoke to each other since their conversation about the jumper she was knitting. She greeted him with a curt nod and went on scouring the pan. She was aware of what a fright she must look. Her dress was crumpled and unironed and she hadn't bothered to comb her hair when she got up that morning. It annoyed her to think that his presence should make her worry about her appearance. She could feel him looking at her and hovering nearby.

Eventually he said, "You work hard!"

The note of appreciation in his voice irritated her all the more because it also pleased her. "I don't exactly have much choice, do I? Still, if I'm forced to stay here I may as well do something than be bored to death."

He said nothing but shuffled slightly. She could feel his discomfort.

"By the way, any news of the ransom? I suppose you'd know since you're the Big Interpreter. I presume that is your role in all this?"

He looked up at her. He was feeling something stronger than discomfort. It clearly pained him that she spoke to him with such dislike and contempt. *Good,* she thought. *And in any case, how could he expect anything else?*

"We have no news yet. Very soon. I tell you at once."

She did not answer but went on rubbing at the pan. Her hands were getting rough and red with all the work she did. She hoped he noticed it, though that was probably how he expected women's hands to look. She was surprised she hadn't already driven him away. The longer he stayed, the more that part of her that longed for friendship recalled her feelings when they had talked together on the beach, before he had betrayed her. She wished he'd go away. He reached into his pocket and brought out a sort of stick, which he offered to her.

"I make something for you."

She wiped her hands on her apron and took it from him. She saw that it was a pipe, about the size of a recorder, with a mouthpiece and holes for stops. It was decorated all over with a carved pattern of leaves.

"It is for you to play. When your work is finished."

Fleur grimaced. He *would* put it like that. "Thank you. It's nice of you," she said stiffly.

He smiled. "I go now," he said, and was gone.

Fleur turned the pipe over in her hands. It was a lovely thing. It must have taken him hours to make. She had some idea how to play it from her memories of playing the recorder in her Welsh school. She put it to her lips and blew, and produced a shrill shriek. Then she placed her fingers on the various stops and began to sound out a few notes. The pipe had a pleasant, watery tone. For several minutes she tried it out. Then she heard Mama's returning footsteps and quickly stuffed it into her pocket and went back to scouring the pan. Mama looked at her curiously. Fleur blushed under her gaze. Mama's face hardened into a frown which then broke up into laughter. She nudged

Fleur playfully and took the milk pan from her, replacing it with a bowl of chestnuts. Sometimes when she was in a good mood like this, despite everything Fleur felt almost happy in her company.

As soon as she had finished, Fleur went off to her room to try her pipe. Her fingers were clumsy and stiff from all the work she did, and at first she found it hard to get the notes properly, especially at the top and bottom of its register. Squeaks and breathy wheezes were often all she got. But in a little while she had worked out the fingering and how to get a whole range of other notes by placing her tongue and lips against the mouthpieces in various ways. She was even able to make use of some of the techniques she'd learned during her few weeks on the saxophone. The pipe had a full, reedy resonance that reminded her a little of Mama's singing. She must have practised for over an hour before she heard Mama calling, "Flora!" She put the pipe away and went back into the kitchen.

During the next few days her pipe grew to be an obsession. She practised it whenever she had a free moment. First she tried simple tunes which she remembered, like hymns and nursery rhymes. Then as she grew more skilled, she started experimenting, trying out snatches of tunes she half-remembered, improvising. She'd always loved music and there was no other source of music around, no radio or record player. But it wasn't just that. The pipe was also a way of talking, of letting out some of the feelings that she had no words to express and no one to understand them even if she had. Soon it wasn't enough just to play a tune correctly. She wanted the pipe to sing to her command, effortlessly like the wind through the olive trees. And she bent all her concentration to achieving the effect. Mama got quite annoyed at her endless practising because it distracted her from her chores. But she was also glad that Fleur took such pleasure in Paulo's gift, and he himself was visibly pleased at its success. Playing her pipe became something not just that Fleur enjoyed doing, but a sort of barrier that she could put up at will between her and the world. It made her forget her fears for a while, and at the same time through it she could reach beyond the confines of the present, her enforced silence and imprisonment.

One evening the supper was cooking and Fleur and Mama were waiting for the men to come home. They were later than usual. Mama was patching a pair of Ermano's trousers and Fleur went to sit by the window to watch the last of the sun disappear behind the darkening mountains. It was always the worst hour of the day, just before darkness fell, the time when it was hardest not to think of home. She took her pipe out of her pocket and started to play, concentrating on the notes and letting the music say what she had no other way of expressing. A few moments later she became aware that Paulo had entered and was standing in the open doorway, listening. She stopped playing at once, feeling suddenly very exposed. He came into the room, closely followed by his brothers.

They hung their jackets and leather satchels on the pegs by the door but instead of sitting down at the table, Ermano went to the wall and took down a stringed, zither-like instrument that habitually hung there but which no one so far had touched. He sat down, put it across his knee, and started to pluck and tune it. Paulo went to the chest and took out a flute, larger and more elaborate than Fleur's, and he and Jesu brought up chairs close to Ermano. Ermano began to pick out a tune on the zither slowly, note by note, then in little runs. Paulo blew a few notes on his flute, harmonising with Ermano, then breaking off, then picking up the tune again. Jesu had produced two blocks of wood which he started to clap together in a rhythmic beat.

Suddenly, with one accord, they took off in a lively tune at a swift tempo. Ermano played the main tune whilst Paulo dipped and danced around him on the flute. Then they swapped round and Paulo took over the tune, with Jesu all the while keeping up the rapid rhythm on his blocks of wood, sometimes knocking them against his hand, his elbow or even his knee. Mama got up from her seat to watch them. She stood with her hands on her broad hips, swaying slightly to the music, a bright, intent expression on her face. Then she put back her head, exposing her strong throat, and started to sing. Her voice was thrilling, sending prickles of excitement down Fleur's spine and making the hairs on her arms rise like goose-flesh. In and out of the players it wove like another instrument.

Fleur listened to them, entranced. The more they played, the more daring and intricate their playing grew. It was so infectious that, scarcely aware of what she was doing, she put her pipe to her lips and sounded out a few notes, fitting them in here and there with the wild tune. Then, in a burst of confidence, she plunged in, making it up as she went along, kept afloat by the powerful rhythm, finding by instinct which notes to play. She never could have done it if she'd stopped to think. *Like the man,* she thought afterwards, *who couldn't swim but he'd been thrown into the pool when drunk and had swum like a fish. And the following morning when he'd tried it again, sober, he'd sunk to the bottom like a stone.* Now somehow or other she kept pace with them, thinking of nothing but the thrill of the music and the woman's voice, which curled and twined around it like smoke as she rocked her great body in a solemn dance.

At last the tune came to an end and they all fell back, out of breath and laughing. Mama's eyes shone and the men's faces were bright with an expression she had never seen on them before. Mama clapped her hands joyfully, then motioned the men over to the table and beckoned Fleur to the range. They brought the food and sat down. The meal of wine stew, chestnut cakes, bread, fruit and goat cheese was a feast that evening. Everyone was in good humour and ate with relish. Mama sat in her place at the head of the table, telling stories and making her sons laugh, and Fleur, despite her silence, felt for once that she was included in their merriment and that her presence did not act as a damper on the occasion. The music had somehow released a tension between them, or at least it had provided something in which at last she too could share. She felt a great relief, as though a terrible burden had for a while been taken from her.

When they had eaten and drunk their fill, they sat back in their chairs and nobody moved from the table. A quiet contentment hung in the air, hovering like the smoke from Ermano's pipe, which filled the room with the scent of mountain herbs. Paulo sat stroking his bitch's head. She had crept from her usual place by the door to be near him, sensing a relaxation of the rules. Fleur stole a look at him. There was something so appealing about his bent head and the way his hair curled in his neck. He looked up, catching her eye, and smiled at her. She smiled back shyly. Nobody spoke.

Then, slowly, as when a different channel starts to break in and interfere with the programme you're listening to on the radio, Fleur became aware of a new voice. It was hard and insistent, repeating something over and over again. Mama's voice faded in mid-sentence. Everyone froze, mesmerised by the unseen force.

"*Attention! Ici la police... Vous êtes encerclé!*" it repeated, over and over. Fleur listened, rigid, trying to make sense of it. *Encerclé...* encircled? ...surrounded? ...Police!

The voice stopped as suddenly as it had started. There was a gap of silence.

Then chaos broke out inside the room. Ermano leapt to his feet, kicking back his chair which crashed to the ground. He snatched up his rifle, shouting orders at his brothers. Jesu doused the lamp, slammed the shutters to, locked them, shut the window and took up position beside it with his gun. Paulo raced for his rifle, and he, Ermano and the dog dived out of the back door, running for cover towards the outhouses. Mama followed them to the door, shut and bolted it behind them. Then she seized hold of Fleur, who was standing in the middle of the room as if paralysed, and pushed her into the corner farthest from the window, covering her body with her own. Outside there was a burst of gunfire and an answering volley from the outhouses, followed by more shouting from the amplified voice and more gunfire. Every time a gun went off, a convulsion ran through Fleur's body as she pressed against Mama in her terror. She heard a pane of glass shatter as Jesu drove his rifle through it and between the shutters, and a loud crack as his gun fired. In the distance a man cried out. Only the warmth of the woman's body kept Fleur from screaming out hysterically. Overwhelmed by fear, she could think of nothing but clinging to that body for her very life.

Then, as suddenly as it had begun, the shooting ceased.

In the room they strained their ears to hear what was going on outside. Nobody moved.

A second later another earsplitting volley of gunfire burst out right under the window. Jesu groaned and fell to the floor with a thud. Mama gasped but did not go to him. Heavy booted feet were running in the courtyard. There was a pounding with rifle butts on the door, more shouting, more gunfire. Then with a splintering crash, the door fell in on its hinges.

Torchbeams flashed round the room and in their crossbeams Fleur saw a group of armed *gendarmes* crowded in the doorway. Their captain rapped out an order and they fanned into the room, covering themselves with their outstretched guns.

Fleur could see them now quite clearly in the torchlight. One of them went over to Jesu and prodded him with his boot. The Captain was aiming his gun straight at Mama and Fleur. He shouted at Mama and waved his gun. She did not move. One of his men stepped forward and grabbed her roughly by the arm. She turned on him in fury and for a moment he drew back, hesitating. The Captain repeated his order and the man came forward again and gave her a blow in the side with his rifle butt, then pushed her forward. She stumbled but recovered herself and, drawing herself up to her full height, said something to the Captain in an angry voice. She walked towards him sedately, followed by the man who had struck her. She took down her shawl from a peg near the door and wrapped it round her head and shoulders. The two men guarding her were getting impatient but they didn't lay hands on her.

Fleur flattened herself against the wall. She wanted desperately to fling herself after Mama but she dared not move. Her legs scarcely held her upright and she felt that at any moment she was going to slump to the floor. Her throat was dry but as she saw the door into the courtyard open and one of the *gendarmes* push Mama towards it, she let out a frantic cry. Mama turned at once and made to come back but the Captain barred her way. She called out in her strong voice, *"Flora! Bonne chance, ma petite!"* And then she was gone, hustled off into the night.

Fleur tried to go after her. The Captain moved to catch her as she stumbled. He put a coat that was much too big around her shoulders and led her to the doorway. She heard the sounds of a car driving off slowly in low gear as she came out into the darkness, and saw the long beams of its headlights tilted against the night sky. The Captain tightened his grip and half-carried, half-dragged her to a waiting car. Someone opened the door from inside and the Captain handed her in. He disappeared back into the house for a few moments, then returned and squashed in on her other side. She was shivering now, despite the coat and the crush in the car. She felt as if she had no will of her own left. She listened to the Captain's incomprehensible words but had no interest in anything he or any of the other men might say. It scarcely mattered what they did with her or where they were taking her.

The engine started up, the car revved, turned, and set off down the stony track. Fleur watched the columns of light from the headlamps rise and dip against the horizon as the car bounced its way over the uneven ground. The thought came to her that she was free at last, saved by these armed, sweating strangers. She should have felt grateful, and relieved. But her mind was filled with one dull thought: Mama was gone!

And deeper down, beneath her weariness, a nameless ache reawakened that burrowed and gnawed its way inside her like a mole, a sense of childish loss, older than Wales, frightening and burdensome, that stretched to the very bounds of her conscious memory to a point where life had ceased to be ordered and secure. Mama had been a bulwark against such loneliness. Now she was gone.

7

THE PRODIGAL'S RETURN

They drove through the darkness until they came to a village where there were no signs of life. The Captain ordered the car to pull up at a house which was larger than the others in the village and had the sign of a telephone outside it. One of the *gendarmes* waited in the car with Fleur, whilst the Captain and the driver knocked up the householder and disappeared inside. Fleur must have fallen asleep because she wasn't aware of their returning and was woken some time later by the uncomfortable heat. They were moving again and the man on her left was snoring, jerking momentarily awake with a sudden snort then falling back into a rhythmic purr. The Captain leaned across Fleur and prodded him. He half-opened his eyes in sleepy bewilderment and at once dozed off again. The Captain himself did not sleep but smoked relentlessly, which only added to the unpleasant fug in the car. Dawn was just breaking as they entered the suburbs of a large town. The sky was growing rosy behind tall blocks of flats which stuck up like bad teeth in a deserted wasteland. Yellow morning light was beginning to seep through the mist that drifted low over the fields and patches of waste ground where chickens scratched and a goat or two was tethered. But the dawn did little to revive Fleur. Her body ached with tiredness and she felt as if it was coated with a thin layer of grease.

They entered the city through its bleak suburbs to the more businesslike centre, and pulled up in the forecourt of a modern hotel. Hardly anyone was about yet, just a few workers in blue overalls going to or from work on spluttering motorcycles, and an early shopkeeper sluicing down the pavement in front of his doorway. The Captain heaved himself out of the car and reached down a helping hand to Fleur. She climbed out, dazed by the brilliance of the morning light, and followed him into the foyer. Another *gendarme* brought up the rear. The Captain collected a key from a sleepy desk clerk, who looked as if he was just coming to the end of his night shift, and led the way to the lift. Along an anonymous corridor on the fifth floor he stopped in front of a door like any other, inserted the key, opened the door, and stood aside to let Fleur pass into the room. It was a typical hotel room, clean and totally impersonal. The divan bed had bedside cupboards in the same shiny veneer as the wardrobe and dressing table. There was an easy chair upholstered in the same colourless material as the window curtains and bedspread, toning in with the beige carpet. Through a half-open door, Fleur could see the small bathroom with shower, bidet and lavatory. The corner of the white sheet was turned down and her nightdress lay neatly folded on the pillow. The bed was the one thing that attracted her in all that gleaming, hygienic modernity. She stared longingly at the white sheets.

"It is only five o'clock. You sleep now," the Captain said. "My man outside. Soon father come."

Fleur couldn't be bothered to explain that Mr Taylor wasn't her father. They must mean Mr Taylor. The thought of seeing him soon caused a flicker of excitement to run through her. She was safe at last. Soon she would be going home! But being here still seemed like a dream. For the moment all she wanted was to sleep. The Captain was hovering near the door.

"I'm all right. I just need to sleep for a while," Fleur said.

He nodded and opened the door.

"My man outside," he repeated, hesitated for a moment, then left.

Fleur went straight to the bed, pulled back the sheet and got in without even bothering to take off her grubby dress. She fell at once into a dreamless sleep.

SOME TIME later she was awoken by a knock on the door. She opened her eyes, confused at first by the unfamiliar, anonymous environment. Then she recognised Mr Taylor, who had come into the room and was standing at the end of the bed.

She sat up.

Mr Taylor smiled at her. "Well, my girl, you've given us all quite a fright, I must say! Thank God you're safe and sound! Your mother, Jan, Gillian, Tony. They all send their love, of course. So how are you, my dear? Still in one piece after all your experiences?"

Fleur could feel his nervousness beneath the torrent of words.

"I'm fine now," she said, pulling the sheet up to hide her crumpled dress. "All I needed was some sleep. How *is* my mother? Is she all right?"

"She's fine too. Now that she knows you're safe. The police phoned through to my hotel last night as soon as they'd got you, and I immediately phoned her. She was incredibly relieved. You can imagine. We all were. I can't tell you!"

"Yes, it feels good, I must say. I'm only just beginning to believe it."

"Well, it's true. You can relax now. By this evening you'll be home."

"Great! What a relief! Are Jan and Mrs Taylor still here?"

"No, they went home some time ago. There didn't seem much point in us all staying and the police wanted them out of the way. We've kept in constant touch, of course."

"I'm afraid it's been an awful lot of trouble for you—"

"My dear!" he cut her off, his face clouding over into the expression of exhausted anxiety that took over whenever he stopped smiling, despite his outward cheerfulness. "You know there isn't anything I, any of us, wouldn't have done to get you back safe and sound. You *are* perfectly safe and sound, I take it?"

He watched her for her reaction. She could see the fear

in his eyes. What was it exactly that he was afraid of? That she had been ill-treated, raped perhaps?

"Yes. Quite safe and sound," she said firmly.

The relief showed in his face though she didn't think that his anxieties had been totally dispersed. It made her rather self-conscious the way he kept looking at her. She supposed she must look a dreadful fright, not at all suitable for this clean bed and immaculate hotel room.

"I've ordered you some coffee," Mr Taylor went on in a cheerful tone. "After you've had that and a chance to shower and change — I've got some clean clothes for you, by the way — it'll be time for lunch. I thought we might have a proper lunch and a chat in the hotel before we leave. You're probably hungry?"

"Yes. That sounds nice. What time are we actually leaving?"

"We're booked on the three o'clock plane. But we've got to stop off at the Police Commissioner for a short while first."

"Oh. What does he want?"

"Nothing much. Just a few questions. Most of the investigation can be completed after we get home. It's nothing to worry about."

Excitement was rising in Fleur. At last home was really in sight. In just a few short hours she would be there and she and her mother would be talking over all that had happened. She could hardly wait to be gone.

There was a knock on the door and a maid entered, carrying a breakfast tray with coffee, orange juice and a croissant. Mr Taylor thanked her and took the tray from her. In the doorway she turned and stared back at Fleur before leaving. Fleur shrank under her gaze. It hadn't occurred to her before that she would be an object of curiosity to perfect strangers. The idea was very unpleasant.

"Will I have to see anyone when we get back? Will we be able to go straight home?" she said.

"Yes. There'll be some English detectives travelling with us. They'll see that everything goes smoothly on our arrival, keep the newsmen off our backs."

"Newsmen! What could they possibly want with me?"

"I'm afraid you're big news at the moment, my dear. You know what some papers are like: 'Young Girl Captured by Terrorists,' that sort of thing. But don't worry, it'll die down soon. They never stick to one story for very long, especially if it turns out to have a happy ending."

"Oh, God, I can imagine," Fleur groaned.

"Anyway, eat your breakfast. I'll pour you some coffee."

"Thanks."

The coffee was bitter and insipid but she was glad of it all the same, and she wolfed down the croissant realising that she was hungry after all.

"I'll leave you to finish, then have a shower and dress. See you downstairs in what, forty-five minutes?"

"Fine."

"OK." He got up. "I can't tell you how happy it makes me to have you back with us again." He leaned forward and pressed her arm, then went to the door. "Take your time. There's no rush." He smiled at her more genuinely than he had at first been able to manage, and left the room.

"Poor man!" she thought. She supposed that everyone would have the same dark thoughts about what had been done to her in captivity. It didn't seem to occur to him that Mama and her sons might have been decent, honourable people in their own way. She was going to have to explain that when she felt a bit more used to being back in the world, and a bit more able to deal with it.

After lunch in the hotel, a police car arrived to take them to the Commissioner. Bewildered as she felt by the abrupt change from one world to another, a shower, fresh clothes and a meal in a restaurant was beginning to make Fleur feel like a new person. Until she saw that outside the hotel a small crowd had gathered, mostly journalists with cameras. The two policemen pushed them aside and hurried her and Mr Taylor into the waiting car, which drove off at high speed. Fleur found the persistent hurling of questions in several languages and popping of flash bulbs from a crowd of strangers, whose interest she felt to be largely predatory, very unnerving. But here at least she didn't understand their questions. At home it would be different. She hoped that Mr Taylor was right when he said that they had been able to calm the press down.

They arrived at the Police Station and were greeted by the Commissioner. He was a short, immensely polite Frenchman in an immaculate uniform. He spoke very good English which he obviously liked to practise as much as possible. Whenever Mr Taylor spoke to him in French, he replied in English. His manner to Fleur was concerned and fatherly.

"We are so 'appy to find you safe and well. It is not

always that these incidents turn out so fortunate. Your fazer say you 'ave not been mistreated. Can this be true?"

"Oh, yes. Quite true. In fact they were very good to me in all—"

The commissioner cut her off with a charming smile of disbelief. "I do not think the word 'good' is one we may use about such people. They are gangsters and terrorists and shall be treated as such."

"No, honestly, you don't understand…" Fleur began.

The Police Commissioner's expression was hardening.

Mr Taylor put his hand on Fleur's arm. "We haven't got long before the plane goes," he said to her quietly. "Let him ask his questions. We can sort the rest out later."

It wasn't going to be easy to convince them. The thought was very depressing. She gave up reluctantly.

The Police Commissioner went on to ask her about how many people there were at the farm and if they had ever had any visitors. He was intensely interested to hear about the two strangers who had come that Sunday, and made Fleur give a detailed description of them which he wrote down.

"That is good," he said. "It will 'elp us find these criminals and to bring them to justice. One, at least, is already dead, two more in custody. They will all get their just deserts. We shall see to it." He put out his hand to Mr Taylor, then turned to Fleur. She could hardly bear to meet his eye let alone take his hand after what he had said concerning Mama and Paulo. But she shook it and murmured a thank you and goodbye. The Commissioner smiled at her kindly.

"Cheer up. It is all over now. Soon you can forget

about zese terrible weeks. And, who knows, perhaps one day you will return to a Corsica freed from such people, to enjoy its sun and hospitality without fear or bad memories. Let us hope so."

His words struck a chill to Fleur's heart. She smiled weakly, avoiding his eye, and walked close to Mr Taylor, as they left the Police Station.

The Commissioner had provided them with a car and an escort to the airport, who were waiting for them outside. There was also another crowd of people, or perhaps the same ones who had followed them from the hotel. They were shoved aside even more brusquely than before, and the car with Fleur and Mr Taylor inside roared off at once, siren blaring, followed by another car with two plain-clothes and one uniformed policeman.

At the airport they were met by the English detectives, waiting to usher them onto the plane ahead of all the other passengers. A section of the first class compartment had been reserved for them to travel in style. The detectives were big, good-humoured men in crumpled, baggy summer suits, who seemed to regard the whole trip as a bit of a holiday. They were already on very good terms with the stewardesses, and when Fleur and Mr Taylor had been shown to their seats, she could hear them all laughing and joking together a few rows in front.

She sat next to Mr Taylor in the window seat.

"Not long now," he said, pressing her arm reassuringly. "You'll soon be able to relax."

He obviously felt more relaxed himself because no sooner had the plane left the runway than he fell into a deep sleep. Fleur glanced at his face. He looked exhausted, almost drained of colour beneath his tan. It was obvious that he had been under a terrible strain. She looked out of the window again at the vanishing island, growing smaller and smaller beneath her until there was no more sign of land at all, only the empty sea. Where were Mama and Paulo now? Were they in some terrible, dank prison cell? She was very afraid for them. Whatever they were guilty of, they mustn't be harmed. If only she could get someone to listen to her, then they might understand that Mama and Paulo were not really criminals, that they had looked after her, protected her. But who would listen? The whole unstoppable machinery of the law, with its police and courts and judges, had already started. How could she break in to tell them what she knew? Was anyone even interested in hearing the truth unless it exactly coincided with the ideas they already had?

She felt a light pressure on her arm and a soft voice asked whether there were anything she wanted. She turned to find herself looking straight into the blue eyes of the steward, his handsome face only inches away from hers.

Startled, she looked away, murmuring, "No, thanks."

It came as a shock to remember how perfect strangers looked at one another with such intimacy. Paulo had never looked at her like that. If he had, she would have known that it wasn't a compliment but more a sign of disrespect. Funny how her view of things had altered over the last few weeks. Would it all wear off in a couple of days and be totally forgotten? She had no clear sense any longer of who she was. She felt caught and suspended between two worlds, belonging in neither.

There were certain things that she didn't want to forget, even when she was back home and settled in to her proper life. For a moment she was filled with a great sadness, a nostalgia for what she already no longer wanted, yet at the same time still regretted. All the time at the farm she had dreamt of this moment when she would be set free and on her way home. Now things didn't seem so simple. She wanted something of both worlds, although she knew that wasn't possible. They seemed contradictory, incompatible. The modern world destroyed the other, older one whenever it came in contact with it, so the other, older world fought for its life. You couldn't straddle them both. You had to choose one or the other, or perhaps not choose because you were either born in one or the other and there was very little you could do about it.

At least soon she would see her mother, and the thought of that was an enormous relief. She would be able to put her fears at rest, to comfort her for all the unhappiness she had caused her. It was strange how responsible for her mother she'd always felt, almost as if she were the mother and her mother the child. In the past this had sometimes seemed a great burden. She'd longed for the sort of mother you read about in storybooks, big and warm and strong and safe — a bit like Mama in fact. But now she didn't mind so much that her mother was more like a friend or a sister than a mother. In fact, she could begin to see it as quite an advantage as she grew older and didn't need someone to look after her so much. It would become easier and easier for them to be friends.

My Taylor woke and looked about him with a startled

air, as if he'd been caught out doing something he shouldn't.

"Everything all right?" he said vaguely.

"Fine." She smiled at him. "I was just thinking how strange it will be, going home, I mean. I'm longing to be back but also I'm a bit afraid of it. Silly, isn't it?"

"It's perfectly natural. Don't worry, you'll soon adjust. Then this whole nightmare will be behind you."

"More of a dream than a nightmare."

It was good to have Mr Taylor beside her. She'd always liked him and even if he didn't quite understand, she felt that he'd be prepared to listen whenever she felt ready to talk.

They had no sooner eaten the light meal the stewardesses served, than their imminent arrival at Heathrow was announced. Fleur heard it with excitement in the pit of her stomach. Nearly home! Yet in another way she needed more time to adjust to all these changes of place and people. They seemed to be flashing before her like things seen on a video when someone puts it on fast forward. She couldn't take them in. As the plane taxied up the runway, the detectives came to tell them to get ready because they were going to be taken off first. The detectives had suddenly assumed a dignified and sober air more appropriate to their responsibility. They led Fleur and Mr Taylor down the steps of the aircraft, along a portable corridor like the corrugated entrails of a huge beast, and into the V.I.P. lounge. There they had to stand about whilst the detectives sorted out their luggage and talked to passport and custom officials. Mr Taylor went off to telephone that they'd arrived safely. It was very quiet in the heavily carpeted V.I.P. lounge and everybody talked in subdued voices. Beyond its walls Fleur could make out the distant hubbub of the packed hall where the ordinary passengers congregated, awaiting their luggage and their loved ones. There was no one there to meet them and she couldn't help feeling disappointed. The detectives said that they'd advised her mother to wait at home in order to avoid reporters.

"They might be a bit rough on you for a few days. But don't worry. They'll soon get tired and go on to someone else," they said.

From the V.I.P. lounge they were whisked into a limousine and sped away in the direction of London. No one spoke much, as if they were in suspended animation awaiting the end of the journey. The mutilated country-side along the motorway looked tired and moth-eaten. Soon it gave way altogether to the more verdant richness of suburban gardens, bursting with summer roses, and then the flyover and the city proper.

Hammersmith was in the throes of a heatwave. The air was close and stuffy after the drier heat of Corsica. The streets were grubby, littered and swarming with life: people scantily clad in shorts and teeshirts or light summer dresses, tired mothers pushing hot, crotchety babies in pushchairs, office workers in shirtsleeves, old people moving slowly on bad feet made worse by the heat, tramps still in their layers of winter rags and news-papers, heads down, shuffling between the crowd as if they had somewhere to go. A group of sleek young black boys on roller-skates, wearing only shorts and head-bands, swept past, weaving in and out of the walkers with perilous grace. Fleur watched them go and suddenly she was filled with a sense of the vitality of this city. London, she realised, was home to her now. Though she belonged there no more than four-fifths of the rest of its population, nevertheless it was her city. It was exciting as well as sordid, and full of energy if also, at times, ugly and brutal.

The car turned into a side street and she recognised her own peeling terrace. They pulled up outside the house and one of the detectives jumped out, ran up the steps and rang the doorbell. The door was opened at once and there, festive in a white dress, anxiously searching for a glimpse of her lost child, stood Fleur's mother. She ran down the steps as Fleur climbed out of the car, and they rushed into each other's arms. For a moment they stood there on the pavement hugging then holding each other at arm's length, half-crying, half-laughing for joy.

Then the senior detective said, "You'd better get inside. We may have been followed."

At that very moment a car veered into the terrace from the far end, one of its passengers leaning perilously out of a side window, camera poised.

"Quick, get in! I'll deal with them," the detective said, and pushed Fleur and her mother towards the open front door.

They entered the house, followed by Mr Taylor and the junior detective, who shut the door firmly behind them.

"What must it be like to be Mick Jagger or Princess Di?" Fleur's mother said and giggled.

"Awful!" Fleur said, and they filed upstairs.

"Isn't it nice to be famous?" the detective said, bringing up the rear.

"You must be joking! I just hope they all clear off soon," Fleur replied.

"After the press conference things usually die down pretty quickly," the detective said.

"Press conference! Who, me? No way!"

"Well, it usually helps to..."

"Does she have to?" Fleur's mother asked.

"Well, it might be possible to give out a statement on your behalf, something that'll satisfy them for the time being. Appeal to their better instincts. It sometimes works."

"Let's give it a try," Fleur's mother said.

"Oh, please," Fleur pleaded.

"All right. We'll see what we can do."

They had reached the front door of the flat. Fleur entered staring round at its shabby familiarity. Everything looked the same as she remembered it, only a little tidier than usual. On the table in the sitting room was a big bowl of moss roses, whose scent filled the room. The sofa was free from its usual pile of newspapers and half-sewn garments, and over the back of it were draped a pair of smart white trousers and a couple of teeshirts in pretty ice cream colours, the shop labels still attached to them. Fleur turned to her mother and, linking an arm in hers, pressed against her. They were exactly what she liked, perfect for the hot weather.

Her mother offered Mr Taylor and the detective the choice of a drink or a cup of tea. The detective declined either, saying that he wasn't allowed to drink on duty and was awash with tea from the plane. Mr Taylor accepted a whisky. In a few minutes they were joined by the senior detective.

"I've seen them off for the time being," he said. "I don't think you'll be bothered again tonight but don't answer the door just in case. I've brought your case up, by the way."

"Thanks," said Fleur.

"That's very kind of you," her mother said.

They stood around chatting gaily, rather as if they were at some sort of cocktail party. Everyone was in such light spirits now that the nightmare was over. Fleur felt so relaxed she kept beaming at people for no reason at all and her mother was almost as giggly as she got after a couple of drinks, though no alcohol had passed her lips as far as Fleur knew. Even the detectives seemed to be infected by the general mood of hilarity. But eventually the senior one got up and said they'd better be on their way.

"We've got to turn in a report at the station before we're finished. We'll be in touch tomorrow. There's one or two things we need to clear up with the young lady. Nothing much, and there's no need for any of you to come down to the station. Best if you lie low for a couple of days. You too, sir."

"There's nothing I'd like better," Mr Taylor said.

The detectives and Mr Taylor shook hands, then Fleur's mother saw them down to the street door. Fleur went and sat down on the sofa. Without thinking she stroked the worn velvet that was now only a faded reminder of its original cornflower blue. She had played and bounced on this sofa all her life, pounding its springs and stuffing almost out of existence. She had a great affection for it.

"Good to be home?" Mr Taylor said.

"I'll say!" There was a pause, then she added, "It's hard to believe that only a few hours ago we were in Corsica, isn't it? And only the night before that… And now we're here! It doesn't seem real."

The anxious weariness came back into his face. "Best to let it all fade away into unreality," he said.

"Oh, I don't want it to fade. Not entirely, now that I'm safe."

"You're very brave. I want to tell you how I admire the way you've come through this. You know how bad I feel."

She blushed with embarrassment. She felt such a fraud. Here he was, thinking of her as some sort of heroine, when in fact she hadn't been brave at all.

"I know you don't believe me, but I really *didn't* have such a terrible time. I wasn't ill-treated. There were even things I almost enjoyed."

He smiled wryly, as if he knew better than she did how terrible her ordeal had been, but was grateful for her comfort. "You persist in seeing it all as some kind of adventure? Well, that's certainly one way of looking at it, and a very positive one." He laughed in self-deprecation. "Funny, all my years in politics didn't prepare for a situation like this. I've felt so completely useless. There's always something to learn, isn't there?"

"Yes," she said smiling at him.

Perhaps one day she could convince him that she hadn't been in the hands of a group of fanatical maniacs, as everyone seemed to think, but with a family of people who, though different from themselves in all kinds of ways, were nevertheless just ordinary people struggling for what they felt to be their survival.

Fleur's mother came back into the room.

"Well, those detectives seem nice enough fellows. They're going to do all they can to keep us out of the lime-light. I think we need a drink. Shall I open a bottle of wine?"

"Not for me, thanks. I'd better be on my way. Gillian'll be wondering where I am. I managed to phone her from the airport and told her that I'd be coming straight home after I'd seen Fleur safely delivered," Mr Taylor said.

"In that case we mustn't keep you. Thank you very much for all you've done for us."

Fleur's mother went up to him and took both his hands in hers. He looked down, overcome with emotion. Then he rallied and said, "Please, it was the least I could do. After all, I was partly responsible."

"You mustn't think that. Anyway, it's all done with now. Soon we must meet up for a real celebration. Perhaps you could all come over for supper next week? We'd like that, wouldn't we, Fleur?"

Fleur nodded and smiled.

"Next week it is, then," he said cheerfully. "I'll get Gillian to call you and set a definite day."

"Oh, and would you tell Jan I'll call her tomorrow, please?" Fleur said.

"I will indeed. I know she's dying to hear from you." Suddenly, he bent down and kissed her on the cheek, then moved quickly away to the door. "I'll be off then. Don't bother to see me down."

He smiled at them again then disappeared down the stairs. They went to the window and watched him emerge from the house, down the steps into the street, and head off, walking quickly, towards the main road. He looked back once, saw them in the window and waved, then disappeared round the corner. They came back into the sitting room.

"Poor man! It's been rough on him. He's taken his responsibility hard," Fleur's mother said.

"He finds it hard to believe that I wasn't raped and tortured."

Her mother put her arm round her and hugged her to her. "But you weren't, were you?"

"You know I wasn't."

"You're right." She let go of her and added, "Hang the wine! What I really fancy is a nice cup of tea. How about you?"

Fleur laughed. "Now I really know I'm home! Yes, I'll make it."

Together they went into the kitchen and whilst Fleur made tea, her mother put a pan of fat on to heat and began to pound bits of chopped parsley and garlic into a lump of butter.

"What are we having?" Fleur asked. "I'm starving. The food on the plane was revolting."

"Good, because there's enough here for an army. It's steak cooked in garlic butter, with chips and salad. I thought you might not have had a decent meal in a long time."

"Great!" She began to gather knives, forks and plates to set the table. "Is Frank coming tonight?"

"No. I decided we'd prefer to be on our own. He phoned earlier to say Welcome Home, though."

"That's nice of him," Fleur said, and for once she meant it. Since he wasn't going to be there that night, she could afford to be generous. Besides, he wasn't really so bad.

When supper was ready they took the telephone receiver off the hook, and sat down to eat. There were four white candles placed around the roses in the centre of the table. Their light flickered on the dull sheen of the best white damask table cloth, and glinted off their wine glasses and the polished cutlery. The steak was delicious, and when they had cleared the plates away, her mother brought in a fruit salad and some homemade blackberry ice cream. Fleur's mother ate little, but sat watching her daughter with satisfaction.

When she was incapable of cramming in another morsel, Fleur sat back in her chair and gave a sigh of fulfilment.

"That was great, Mum! God, it's good to be home!"

Her mother smiled happily. "Anyone would think you hadn't eaten for a week!"

"Actually, that was one thing we did do well. Mama was a great cook."

"Mama?"

"That's what I called her. It was the only name I ever heard her called, so eventually I called her it too."

"And what was she like, this Mama?"

"She was nice. A bit strict, but nice. She was a big woman, you know, strong and quite tough even though she was quite old. Sometimes she got angry, but she had a good sense of humour and she never actually mistreated me. Sometimes she stood up for me. She called me Flora. She could sing too."

"She doesn't sound too bad, considering."

"Yes, I suppose I grew quite fond of her in a way. She was good to me, really."

"And what about the others?"

"Her sons? I didn't like them much. Except Paulo. He was the youngest. He was nice, despite everything. I've never met a boy like him before. I wish things could have been different."

She paused in thought and her mother continued to watch her. Then she went on, "But I couldn't imagine him away from Corsica. He'd be lost over here, degraded somehow. Even more lost than I was over there."

Her mother nodded.

"I just can't bear to think of them in prison. What do you think'll happen to them?"

"It said in the paper that two of the men had been captured and were awaiting trial. The woman will probably be allowed to go free."

Tears of relief gathered in Fleur's eyes. She closed them, seeing for a moment a vivid image of Mama, head thrown back, strong throat working as she sang in her deep strange voice one of those harsh, haunting songs. She had a feeling that would have been homesickness, except that here she was, back at last in her real home and only too glad to be so. She opened her eyes again, pushing the memory from her.

"And what about Paulo? He isn't eighteen yet. Surely he won't have to spend the rest of his life in prison?"

"If he's as young as that, maybe they'll deal fairly leniently with him —a year or so's detention perhaps, then probation."

"I hope you're right. He wasn't really bad. I don't think any of it was his fault. He was just following orders. I doubt he had much choice."

She thought for a moment, then went on, "Mr Taylor says they're all in it. The Freedom Movement, I mean. He said unless you get the ring leaders, if you punish one, you really ought to punish the whole population. And they never seem able to catch the leaders."

"I suppose the trouble with finding the ring leaders is that if everyone's in it, or at least sympathetic, no one will talk. And even if they aren't involved, they'd probably be afraid to talk," said her mother.

"What d'you think's happened to them to make them so angry and bitter? It must have been something terrible."

"No doubt it was. Centuries of violence and brutality. Corsica was always being invaded, wasn't it? But that doesn't justify further violence. It has to stop somewhere, otherwise it will go on forever."

"I know. All the same, I don't think it's right to call Mama and Paulo, even Ermano, gangsters and terrorists. Whatever I thought of them at the beginning."

"Well, people are often pretty quick to label others. And the labels rarely fit when you get to know them."

Fleur thought at once of Mrs Miller at school. She was a great one for labels. The thought of Mrs Miller failed to arouse the usual feelings of anger and frustration. School seemed so far away with all its petty battles. She wasn't going to get drawn into those again.

"Perhaps in the end some good'll come of all this," Fleur said.

"Good?"

"Yes. Things seem different to me now. I can feel more what's important."

Her mother smiled. "Well, I'm glad of that."

"It isn't that I ever want to go back to Corsica, but I want it to go on being there, to know that *they'll* go on being there. Forever."

"Yes."

Fleur felt that her mother understood though it was hard to find words for what she meant. She knew that it was very important not to forget what had happened, what it had really been like, not to let the stories that she would tell and that other people would expect from her, take over from the truth. She wished she had something to help her remember, some snapshots or souvenir. But she had nothing.

Then suddenly she remembered her pipe. In all the turmoil of the last twenty-four hours she had forgotten it. If the police had retrieved her beach bag from the farm and given it to Mr Taylor, then it might contain the pipe. And the bag might be in her suitcase that was still standing in the hall.

She got up quickly from the table and hurried out. In the hall, she laid the suitcase flat on the floor and opened it up. At first she could see nothing, but then, rummaging down one side, her fingers touched the smooth plastic surface of her beach bag. She pulled it out, opened it and felt about inside. Beneath the still damp towel, she felt two hard objects. One was her comb, the other the pipe. She pulled it out excitedly and held it up to the light, examining it for damage. To her joy there was no flaw in the delicate surface of carved leaves. She ran back to her mother.

"Look, Mum. My pipe! Paulo made it for me."

Her mother stopped clearing the table and took the pipe from her outstretched hand. She looked at it carefully before handing it back.

"It's beautiful. It must have taken him a long time to make," she said.

"He's clever, isn't he?"

"Very. Can you play it?"

"Yes. Would you like to hear me?"

"Very much."

Her mother sat down again and composed herself to listen. Fleur blew a few notes, nervously trying to regain the feel of her fingers and lips on the pipe. It wasn't more than a few hours since she'd played but it felt like years. She ran up and down the scale a couple of times then, suddenly regaining her confidence, she began to play. She had chosen, without thinking, the song that Mama had sung that evening when she, Fleur and Paulo sat alone together in the firelight. She remembered it perfectly, as if the notes had imprinted themselves on her memory. The music sang forth from the pipe and hung on the air in a cascade of pure, full sounds that recalled unforgettably all that was most precious to her about that distant, lonely place.

When she had finished, her mother sat back in her chair and clapped her hands together.

"That was beautiful, darling!"

Fleur beamed with pleasure. "And it isn't very loud, is it? Perhaps it will be all right for me to practise here?"

"I should think so. Not even the neighbours could really object to this. It won't get you a place in the school band, though."

"I don't mind that. It's not the sort of instrument that goes with the music they play. I can play this at home. I'd still like to take up the saxophone again, though. I could do that at school, and the pipe here. It'd be good to have both."

Her mother smiled. "Yes," she said.

READ THE SEQUEL

A CORSICAN TALE

Over twenty years later, Fleur, now known by her middle name, Jessie, decides to revisit Corsica to confront the ghosts that continue to haunt her. *A Corsican Tale* tells the story of this journey, and of her meeting with people and events that bring about change and life lessons in love and the healing power of forgiveness.

A SHORT HISTORY OF CORSICA

The island of Corsica, a gem set in a glittering blue sea, has a turbulent history. Its position has always made it an object of desire to surrounding nations, for whoever controlled Corsica could dominate the Western Mediterranean. For the island and its people, this meant centuries of war and strife, invasion and occupation.

In earliest times the invaders were Greeks, Carthaginians and Romans; in the Dark Ages, Vandals and Ostrogoths; at the time of the Crusades, the Saracen raiders. Even in comparatively peaceful times, the feudal lords quarrelled among themselves and their rule over the people was harsh and oppressive.

In desperation the people appealed to the Pope, who sent Lodolphe, the Archbishop of Pisa in Italy, to govern the island. Under the Pisan administration during the 12 th and 13 th centuries there was relative calm. But the power of Pisa was soon challenged by another Italian city state, Genoa, resulting in constant battles in which the Corsican feudal lords frequently changed allegiance.

The Genoese eventually gained the upper hand and ruled Corsica from 1347 until the late 1700s. They proved harsh overlords, who exploited the land even worse than the feudal lords. The Corsican hero Sampiero led an uprising against them, but they killed him and redoubled their harsh rule. The people suffered bitterly from excessive taxation, famine and poverty. Hunger and desperation forced many to emigrate to the Continent.

In 1729 a guerrilla war of independence began, and the Corsicans asked for help from the French. With the cooperation of one of the most enlightened men ever to rule the island, Pascal Paoli, they finally gained control of it, and Paoli remains a popular hero to this day. Eventually, however, he fell out with the French rulers and created a brief allegiance with the British and Lord Nelson, (who lost his eye at the siege of Calvi during the French Revolutionary Wars). But in 1796 Paoli and the British were ousted, and the island fell to the French. Napoleon, a Corsican from Ajaccio, became the conqueror of Europe, and to this day French remains the official language of Corsica.

Over the years the feeling has grown that the French have ignored the loyalty of the Corsican people through two World Wars, and neglected their responsibility towards them. In the Second World War, the island was occupied by 80,000 Italians, with the help of 10,000 Germans, and as a result the town of Bastia was bombed by both the Germans and the Allies. But the Corsicans remained loyal to the French. They had a strong partisan movement, who maintained contact with the Free French, and the guerrilla tactics learned during this period continued to serve the Independence Movement after the war ended.

In 1962 at the end of the Algerian War, the French government allotted considerable portions of Corsican land to ex-colonialists (pieds noirs) who wished to leave Algeria. This added to the Corsican people's sense of injustice, of being treated as a colony to be exploited according to the whim of their masters. Corsicans continued to be forced into economic exile, as the fight for a still unrealised independence intensified.

ALSO BY JANE CORBETT

The Last Musketeer

Looking for Home

Beasts and Lovers

ABOUT THE AUTHOR

Jane Corbett studied English at Newham College, Cambridge, and is the author of a YA novel *Out of Step*, a volume of modern fairy tales titled *Beasts and Lovers*, and several award-winning screenplays. In the seventies she taught at the progressive Kingsway College, including among her students John Lydon and Timothy Spall. Now, she runs workshops for writers and filmmakers and teaches documentary filmmaking at the National Film and Television School. Her other passions are horse riding, yoga and her grandson. She lives in London with her husband.

www.janecorbett-writer.com

www.ingramcontent.com/pod-product-compliance
Lightning Source LLC
Chambersburg PA
CBHW030835200726

48285CB00007B/2447